# Brainboy AND THE
# DEATHMASTER

# Brainboy AND THE DEATHMASTER

## TOR SEIDLER

LAURA GERINGER BOOKS

*An Imprint of* HarperCollins*Publishers*

The author would like to thank
Brad Arlett and Juan Gamboa
for their help in matters scientific.

Brainboy and the DeathMaster
Copyright © 2003 by Tor Seidler
For information address HarperCollins Children's Books, a division of
HarperCollins Publishers, 1350 Avenue of the Americas, New York, NY 10019.
www.harperchildrens.com
Library of Congress Cataloging-in-Publication Data
Seidler, Tor.
Brainboy and the DeathMaster / Tor Seidler.—1st ed.
p.   cm.
Summary: When Darryl, a twelve-year-old orphan, is adopted by a technology
genius, he finds himself the star of his very own life-threatening video game.
ISBN 0-06-029182-6 (lib. bdg.) — ISBN 0-06-029181-8
[1. Orphans—Fiction. 2. Video games—Fiction. 3. Science fiction.] I. Title.
PZ7.S45526 Bp 2003                                        2002033918
[Fic]—dc21                                                      CIP
                                                                AC
Typography by Alicia Mikles
1 2 3 4 5 6 7 8 9 10
❖
First Edition

*For Milo and Lily*

*For Milo and Lily*

# Brainboy AND THE
# DEATHMASTER

"**D**arryl? Are you awake?"

He was, more or less. He was lying on his back in the bed nearer the window, his eyes closed, but not quite all the way. His focus kept switching back and forth between his crisscrossing eyelashes and a spiderweb in a corner of the ceiling. They looked kind of alike.

"Try and be quiet, Boris," Ms. Grimsley said, lowering her voice. "Darryl's been through a very traumatic experience. He needs his sleep."

"Aw, he's faking it," said a gruff-sounding voice.

Darryl lifted his head slightly and, opening his eyes a bit wider, saw the boy who'd come into the room with Ms. Grimsley. He didn't look so gruff. He was even scrawnier than Darryl, though perhaps a year or two older—thirteen, maybe fourteen. He had a greasy blond ponytail, a tattoo on his arm, and a beat-up backpack over his shoulder.

"Boris is going to be sharing the room with you, Darryl," Ms. Grimsley said. "Do try and make it down to dinner this evening. It's been over a week—time to mix with the others."

Ms. Grimsley left, shutting the door behind her, and Darryl's head sank back onto his pillow. Another fly had gotten caught in the spiderweb, the eighth or ninth new victim since he'd arrived at this place. The spider lurked in the center of the web, biding his time. Once the fly got tired of struggling, the spider would crawl over and wrap him up for future use.

"Hey, fleabrain. Get off my bed."

Darryl heard the words but didn't really put them together.

"Hey! You deaf?"

Something jabbed Darryl in his side: a smelly running shoe. After a third jab, Darryl got up and flopped down on the other bed, the one farther from the window. He couldn't have cared less which bed he was in.

"Got any money?"

The most recently caught fly had quit fluttering around so much on the edge of the web, and the spider had moved half an inch closer.

"Hey, I'm talking to you, dipwad. You got any money? Or a candy bar or something? I could eat a friggin' horse."

A bell rang, far away: two floors down. Bringing him to this room, Ms. Grimsley had led him up two flights of stairs.

"So what's the food like in this joint?"

In a quick dart, the spider was on the fly.

"Hey, mush-for-brains! I asked you . . . aw, forget it. Touch my stuff and you're dog meat."

The boy dumped his backpack on the bed nearer the window and went off to eat, slamming the door so hard, the spiderweb quivered. This didn't seem to bother the spider, who was methodically turning the fly into another mummy. As the spider spun his silk, rays of the sinking sun bounced off the leaves of the madrona tree just outside the window, sending gold spangles across the room's faded, flower-patterned wallpaper.

After a while the daylight began to die out. Somebody knocked on the door. The plump, swarthy woman in the yellow uniform padded in. She set a tray covered with a cloth on the desk.

"Don't let it go *frío* again. Eat while it's nice and *caliente*."

As soon as she left, Darryl jumped up and opened the window, then flopped back down and pulled the pillow over his head and lay there breathing his own breath. Though it was July, the night air was brisk, and once the room turned cool, he pulled his head out from under the pillow to find that the disturbing chicken-pot-pie smell had dissipated.

Eventually another faraway bell rang. A few minutes later a shaft of light fell into the darkened room.

"Darryl?"

Turning his head slightly, he saw Ms. Grimsley's narrow silhouette in the doorway.

"Do try and be quiet, Boris," she whispered. "Can you get to bed without a light?"

"No problem."

The door closed softly. After about fifteen seconds the fluorescent ceiling light flickered on. Boris whipped the cloth off the tray on the desk.

"Hey, dipwad, don't you want your dessert?"

Boris grabbed the eclair and wolfed it down. Then he sat on the sill of the open window and pulled half a cigarette and a pack of matches out of his sock and lit up, blowing the smoke out into the madrona. When he finished, he flicked the cigarette out into the leaves and fixed his eyes on Darryl.

"You never said if you got any money."

He went over to Darryl's jacket, draped over the back of the desk chair, and dug a pack of chewing gum and the stub of a ferry ticket out of the right-hand pocket. From the left pocket he pulled a small paperback book called *The Expanding Universe.*

"Sounds like a real winner," he said, tossing it on the night table. "You a nerd or something?"

Darryl felt a pinch deep in the center of his chest.

"Hey, this is more like it."

The boy had pulled something from the inside pocket of the jacket. Darryl sprang up and snatched it away.

"Jeez, I wasn't going to kipe it," Boris said resentfully.

Darryl sat back down on his new bed, gripping his GameMaster in both hands.

"You must have dough if you got one of them things. I priced them one time for Nina." Boris's eyes were locked on the GameMaster. "I could unload it for you. They're a cinch to unload. Or if you want it all up front, we could do a swap. You don't dig chocolate? . . . How about red licorice? I'll give you a big bag of Twisters for it."

Darryl stared at the darkened screen above the GameMaster's small keyboard.

"No? Then how about some smokes?"

*Smoke.* Darryl's throat tightened, and so did his grip on the GameMaster.

"Smokes? Okay, I'll be back by wake-up." Boris stuffed his backpack and his pillow under the covers of his bed so it looked as if a body was lying there; then he flicked off the light. "If you don't say nothing, it's a deal. A carton of smokes."

As the boy climbed out the window into the madrona tree, Darryl squeezed his eyes shut, but the image of smoke just became more vivid: smoke rising from the charred skeleton of a house. Panicking, he flicked on the lamp on the table between the beds, and the sudden brightness washed the dark image away. But a faded alpine scene of rugged mountains painted on the lampshade ripped at his insides like fangs. His palms turned oily, and one of his hands slipped, hitting the GameMaster's On button.

As the game list appeared on the screen, his breathing instantly grew calmer. CastleMaster, MasterTrek, StarMaster, StarMaster 2, CyberMaster, MasterJinx . . . His right index finger moved to the roller ball below the little keyboard. He clicked on MasterTrek, and the Rules of the Game started scrolling across the screen:

**The goal of MasterTrek is simple: to get Home. But the trek is not so simple. TIME IS OF THE ESSENCE. You have just one hour to complete your journey, and though you know your destination, you don't know your starting point. To establish your location you must answer five questions correctly. To learn the perils that await you on your journey—nests of space eels, asteroid belts, etc.—you must answer five more questions correctly, then choose the most efficient mode or modes of transportation. If you are deep in an iridium mine on one of the**

**moons of Jupiter, you will need both a drill driver and an armored space shuttle; if you're in a black hole on the edge of the Bellaphus galaxy, you will need a phase 6 space probe or, if attacks seem likely, a phase 4 space probe, which is slower but better armored. . . .**

Darryl had no need to read the rules. He'd played the game hundreds of times. MasterTrek, like all GameMaster games, required manual dexterity, but brainpower was far more crucial, and after his first few attempts he'd always made it home to Earth with minutes to spare. In fact, his secret objective these days was to make it in *half* an hour.

Tonight his starting point was a steamy swamp that turned out to be on the planet Venus. Amazingly near Earth. But even so, he hadn't even reached Earth's moon in his space shuttle when the strange words TIME'S UP! flashed onto the screen, accompanied by an ominous *clunk*.

Darryl jabbed the restart button in disgust.

**I**t was eight-thirty in the morning when he heard a swear word and peered up from a bell-shaped nebula in the Vulpecula galaxy to see his new roommate tumble in the open window and sink down on the other bed, which was scattered with buttery pads of sunlight.

"What a freakin' night! The joker at the 7-Eleven wouldn't sell to me, then this pinhead cop hangs out in the parking lot for like a year and a half. Then I had to bribe this bum who smelled like the back end of a garbage truck." Boris pulled a carton of Marlboros out from under his sleeveless sweatshirt. "But I scored 'em." He tossed the carton onto Darryl's bed and went around behind him. "StarMaster, eh. Jeez, level seventeen! You're like Nina."

Darryl concentrated on negotiating a meteor shower on the outskirts of the distant galaxy. It had been a humiliating night. He'd needed four tries to get home in MasterTrek, and in his first two attempts at StarMaster 2, mental lapses had led to ignominious defeat. It was as if the charge in his brain battery was low. But in this third attempt, he was doing halfway decently, having led his rebel troops in a tricky sling-shot maneuver around the black hole in M87.

He was trying to secure an all-important star gate when the boy snatched the GameMaster out of his hands. Darryl grabbed it back—but too late. It let out a sickening splintering sound as a meteorite shattered his lead troopship.

"Look what you did!"

"So he talks. I thought maybe you was one of them finger geeks. That's mine, you know."

As Darryl shoved the GameMaster under his belt like a gun, Boris's eyes narrowed to almost nothing, siz-ing Darryl up. Then he turned and opened a laptop computer on the desk.

"Ought to try this one."

His first day there Ms. Grimsley had encouraged Darryl to use the laptop, telling him it worked between eight-thirty in the morning and four in the afternoon. But he'd hardly given it a glance.

"Trouble is, they bolt 'em into the desk, and the desk's bolted to the floor. You'd need a freakin' chain saw to get it loose." Boris flicked on the computer and stepped aside to give Darryl a view. The word MondoGameMaster, each letter a different color, flashed onto a screen ten times the size of the one on his GameMaster. Drawn irresistibly to the desk chair,

Darryl hit the enter key. Instead of the game list, a maze appeared on the screen. He'd seen such mazes in puzzle books, with an entrance on one side and an exit on the other, but never one this intricate.

"That's the trouble," said Boris. "You got to get through that thing. And they don't give you no time."

A countdown of seconds was underway in the upper right-hand corner of the screen: 120, 119, 118 . . . All you got were two minutes to pilot the little figure through the maze. But instead of grabbing the mouse, Darryl simply stared at the screen. There were choices at every turning, and there must have been a hundred turnings.

"Come on, brainiac, there's only fifty seconds left," Boris said, whacking Darryl on the back.

Darryl didn't reach for the mouse till the count-down reached thirty. It took him twenty seconds to guide the figure through the labyrinth.

"Way to go!" Boris cried as a new message flashed onto the screen:

**Congratulations! You have earned the right to play any game you wish. Have fun—and do your best!**

This message was soon replaced by the same game list as on Darryl's GameMaster, except here StarMaster

2 had been upgraded to StarMaster 3. Intrigued, Darryl chose that. Familiar rules scrolled across the screen:

**The goal of StarMaster 3 is simple: to save the universe. . . .**

Darryl clicked to the opening game screen, but instead of the usual intergalactic map, three words appeared on the screen.

**Want to play?**

What else would he want to do? But when he clicked on Start again, nothing happened.

"Maybe you got to answer," Boris said.

Darryl shrugged and typed in:

**Who are you?**

The answer popped up immediately:

**HighFlier. Who are you?**

HighFlier was clearly a made-up name, so instead of typing in Darryl Kirby, Darryl typed in his initials, MDK. His full name was actually Martin Darryl Kirby.

**Want to play, MDK?**

As soon as Darryl typed Yes, the map of the universe unfurled on screen.

What he loved about StarMaster was that it required multiple skills. First you had to locate the strongholds of the Controllers and the hideouts of the Individualists, avoiding the Controllers' barrages and picking up the Individualists' radio transmissions. And unlike MasterTrek, StarMaster didn't let you simply ignore the impossibility of exceeding the speed of light. To travel between galaxies, you had to locate wormholes and star gates, always well hidden and jealously guarded. Only when you'd mapped the universe, shading the Controllers' galaxies in red and marking the locations of the Individualists with green dots, could you start enlisting the Individualists' help in overthrowing the Controllers. But the Individualists never risked divulging their hiding places and merging their scrappy troops with yours unless they'd decided you were shrewd enough to conquer the Controllers. So they tested you.

After color-coding the universe, as he almost always managed to do, Darryl contacted his first Individualist leader, who gave him twelve seconds to come up with the square root of 529. It took him five seconds to type in "23." The next one he located gave him sixteen seconds to answer a riddle: What occurs once in a minute, twice in a week, and once in a year? After thinking hard for ten seconds, Darryl typed, "THE LETTER E." The next gave him fourteen seconds to come up with the approximate half-life of uranium 238, which Darryl happened to know was four and a half billion years. The next Individualist asked him an easy one: five seconds to type in the common name for sodium chloride. SALT. But the next was less accommodating, giving him only ten seconds to answer this: How much dirt is in a hole two feet deep, three feet wide, and four feet long? After six seconds Darryl was on the verge of typing in 24 cubic feet, but at the last instant he realized it was a riddle, not a math problem, and typed in "NONE." There was no dirt in a hole.

"What a freakin' whiz!" Boris cried as Darryl snagged his fifth Individualist battalion.

His troops assembled, Darryl attacked one of the Controllers' more poorly defended outposts, using a favorite technique of sending a small force on a direct frontal assault and, once the Controllers were engaged, deploying his main force to attack from the rear. This worked twice. But when he tried it a third time, the Controllers only pretended to engage, and when Darryl initiated his rearguard action, they were ready. Not only did he have to order a full retreat, he lost ten percent of his hard-won rebel army.

"I can't believe it," he muttered. "In my GameMaster

they always react the same way."

"Maybe you're not playing the computer," Boris said. "Maybe that HighFlier guy's a person."

"How could that be?"

"You got me, Einstein."

"It must be the upgrade. They reprogrammed it so it learns."

Darryl started varying his attack strategies. But the Controllers varied their defenses just as skillfully. It was the stiffest resistance he'd ever encountered. Finally, getting desperate, he had to seek out more troops.

One of the few Individualist holdouts posed this question: A Saturnalian snail wants to get out of an iridium mine. The snail manages to crawl up the mine shaft three feet each day, but at night when he rests he slips back down two feet. If the shaft is thirty vertical feet, how long will it take him to get out? Thirteen seconds.

After racking his brain, Darryl typed in 28 DAYS, and—presto—the Individualist joined his force.

"Way to go, brainboy!"

So saying, Boris slid his hand down and grabbed the GameMaster out of Darryl's belt. For a second Darryl was horribly torn. All his instincts were against abandoning the game. But the same instincts revolted against the theft of his beloved GameMaster. Finally he swiveled in his chair. The thief was yanking the pillow and backpack out from under his covers.

"I'm bailing on breakfast," Boris said, slipping the GameMaster under his pillow and flopping down on his bed. "Keep it down, willya?"

Darryl's eyes returned to the computer screen. While his back was turned, the Controllers had mounted a counterattack. He'd never seen anything like it!

But even so, forsaking his GameMaster was more than he could stand.

"It's mine," he cried, jumping up.

"Hey. I said keep it down. Your smokes is right there. That was the deal."

"What deal?"

"What do you think I was doin' all night, cuttin' my freakin' toenails?"

"I don't want any cigarettes. I don't smoke."

"Never too late to start."

Glancing back at the screen, Darryl saw his troops being engulfed by Controllers. It was hopeless.

He grabbed the carton of cigarettes and tossed it onto the other bed. "Give me my GameMaster," he said.

The boy leaped up and pulled something from his pocket. *Click.* A knife blade glinted half an inch from the end of Darryl's nose.

"You gonna shut your pie hole, or am I gonna have to cut you?"

## 3

"**I** do appreciate your help, sugar pie. This is the one that always gets to me—those two long flights of stairs."

"No sweat, Ma."

BJ Walker got out of the car and went around to the trunk and pulled out the bag with the MCS tag pinned to it. It was full of books and videos. His mother worked for the Seattle Public Library, and on Saturdays she took books and videos to a couple of nursing homes, some hospices, and this place: the Masterly Children's Shelter. BJ had started helping her three weeks ago, when his summer vacation started, and on his first visit to the shelter he'd been awed by its grandeur. It was in an old mansion with a huge crystal chandelier at the foot of the front staircase and a paneled dining room with a table big enough for a skateboard course. But once he'd gone from room to room on the second and third floors, collecting old library books and handing out new ones, his awe had turned to pity. He'd always felt unlucky for never having known his father, but the kids here were totally alone in the world—wards of the state, waiting till strangers picked them out. When BJ got back into the car that first Saturday, he leaned over and gave his mother a hug.

"What's that for, sugar pie?"

"Oh, nothing."

The shelter wasn't all that far from their house, and this morning they'd made it their first stop. He said, "Morning," to the plump Mexican-looking woman in the yellow uniform who was setting out boxes of breakfast cereal on the table in the dining room; then he poked his head in the half-open door beyond the stairs. Ms. Grimsley, the boss of the shelter, was in her office, leaning back in her desk chair, reading a paperback. Though around his mother's age, Ms. Grimsley was about as different from her as a person could be, thin and pale and dry as straw, with steel-rimmed glasses and a mouth set in a natural frown. But this morning she didn't look as cheerless as usual. On the cover of her paperback a wavy-haired white guy was crushing a delicate woman in his muscular arms.

"Morning, Ms. Grimsley."

She let out a yelp and nearly toppled over backward. As soon as she steadied herself, she thrust the paperback into a handbag that was hanging off the chair back.

"Sorry, ma'am. Just wanted to give you the new videos."

"Yes, yes, of course. I'll collect the old ones and leave them for you on the hall table. You can go on up—everybody should be awake. Breakfast's in ten minutes."

He gave her this week's videos and headed up the front stairs with the bag of books. The shelter had a high turnover. According to his mother, they tried to place the kids with foster parents as quickly as possible—but the sneering redheaded girl who liked horror stories was still in the first room on the second floor, as was the wild-haired boy with the nose ring next door who didn't "read no books." The third bedroom on the second-floor hallway, empty last week, was now occupied by two Asian boys, clearly brothers, who politely accepted the first two books he offered. The black boy in the next room, who'd liked books about the sea, had been replaced by an Eskimo-looking boy who chose a book about wolves.

There were only a couple of rooms up on the third floor. When he knocked on the first door, no one answered, but he opened it anyway, remembering last week's lodger: a boy who'd lain in bed, totally unresponsive, staring at the ceiling. BJ had actually thought of him a couple of times during the week. Of all the kids in the place, that one seemed the saddest case, the most dazed with grief. He was still there—but today he was sitting up in bed while another boy, a skinny kid with a greasy ponytail, was holding a switchblade to his nose.

"Who the freak are you?" the boy with the knife demanded.

"BJ Walker," BJ said. "Who are you?"

"None of your friggin' business."

BJ stepped in and set his book bag by a laptop on the desk. All the rooms here had laptops. "You guys want something to read?"

"You nuts? Can't you see we're busy?"

"What about you?" BJ asked the other boy.

"Hey," the first boy said, turning the knife on BJ. "You think I'm talking to the friggin' walls? I said get out of here."

"What's that?" BJ asked, shifting his eyes to the window.

As soon as the boy looked that way, BJ had his wrist. He twisted the arm till the elbow was pointing at the ceiling and the knife clunked onto the spiral rug between the twin beds.

"Let go of me!"

"Whatever you say." BJ shoved the scrawny boy facedown onto the bed nearer the window, his head at the foot, and sat on the small of his back.

"Get off me!"

"Put a sock in it," BJ said, smiling at the other boy, who looked about his age, though a lot smaller. His blue eyes were glazed, and his dirty-blond hair was every which way, as if he hadn't combed it all week. "What's your name?"

The boy said nothing.

"Don't you have a name?"

The boy took a deep breath and said: "Darryl."

"Why'd he have a knife on you, Darryl?"

"I don't know."

"Get your black butt off me!" squealed the pinned boy.

"I said put a sock in it. You don't know how come he pulled a knife on you?"

Darryl reached between other boy's running shoes and pulled something out from under the pillow.

"Wow," said BJ, who'd been saving up for a GameMaster for months. "You mean they give them out here?"

"It's mine," Darryl said.

"It's mine!" the other boy squealed. "We had a deal! I got you them cigarettes."

"I don't smoke."

"You're killing me, man! You weigh a friggin' ton."

A bell rang in the distance. Footsteps sounded out in the hall.

"Breakfast time," BJ said. "Hand me that knife, will you?"

Darryl set his GameMaster on the table between the beds, collected the knife off the floor, and gave it to BJ, who closed the blade.

"Surprised they let you in here with something like this. What's your name?"

"What's it to you?" the pinned boy said.

"Just being friendly."

"If you want to be friendly, get your smelly butt off me."

"The only thing that smells around here is your shoes, Nabatw."

"What you call me?"

BJ poked the tattoo on the boy's arm. It was of a flag, but instead of stars and stripes inside, it had the letters NABATW.

"That's not my name."

"What is it then?"

"None of your business."

BJ bounced on him, making him gasp.

"Okay, jeez. Name's Boris."

"If I let you up, Boris, are you going to be nice?"

Boris sniffed. BJ bounced on him again.

"Okay, okay. I'll be nice."

When BJ stood up, Boris jerked into a sitting position, his face scarlet, his smelly shoes wide apart on the rug, his slitty eyes shifting between BJ and Darryl.

"Give it to me," he said, his eyes stopping on BJ.

BJ slid the knife into the pocket of his baggy jeans. "You can get it back from Ms. Grimsley."

"You can't give it to Grimface!"

BJ sat on the bed by Darryl.

"How old are you anyway, Boris?"

"Fourteen."

Pretty runty for fourteen, BJ thought. "Where you from?" he asked.

"What's it to you?"

"Just curious."

"Eugene."

"Oregon?"

"No, Hawaii. What do you think, dipwad?"

"What are you doing up here in Seattle?"

"'Bout six months ago my sister and me got tossed in a place like this down in Portland, but the second morning I come down to breakfast—no Nina. They don't let boys and girls share rooms in these joints, even if they're related. Anyhow, somebody must've done something really crummy to make her take off without telling me."

"You sure they didn't stick her with foster parents?"

"That's what the dorks that run the place said. But Neen wouldn't've gone without telling me. Since then I've been looking for her. I've been to Yakima,

Centralia, Tacoma, all over the friggin' place. Figure she's gotta be somewhere in the Northwest." He dug a worn cowhide wallet out of his back pocket and showed them both a dog-eared photo of a girl who looked a lot like him, except she was kind of pretty and wore glasses and her blond hair was curly. "Seen her?"

"Sorry," BJ said.

"If I had a nickel for every time I heard that," Boris said, "I'd be rich as that Masterly jerk."

"Hey, who are you calling a jerk?"

"What's it to you? Like you know Keith Masterly or something?"

"Well, not personally," BJ admitted. But he knew all about him: how he'd invented the GameMaster when he was only nineteen years old, how he'd founded MasterTech when he was only twenty, how instead of hoarding his billions, he financed charitable causes: hospitals for the mentally challenged and shelters like this one for orphaned or abandoned children.

"What about your parents?" he said. "Are they dead?"

"My mom is," Boris said.

"And your dad?"

Boris spat on the floor. "Far as we're concerned."

"How about you, Darryl?"

Darryl turned and stared out the window.

"He's a space case," Boris said. "But I got to admit, he's a friggin' whiz at that GameMaster stuff. He's as good as Nina."

"Where'd you get your GameMaster?" BJ asked. "You rich or something?"

Darryl didn't respond.

"What's your favorite game?"

At this Darryl seemed to perk up a bit. "StarMaster."

"Never played that. Could you show me how?"

Instead of picking up his GameMaster, Darryl moved to the desk chair. When he hit a key on the laptop, the word MondoGameMaster appeared on the screen, each vibrating letter a different color.

"They're like big GameMasters?" BJ said, moving over behind him. "Is that because Keith Masterly owns this place?"

"I guess," Darryl said. "But it's weird. I think you play against somebody. First you have to get through this maze, though. Huh. It's different this time."

An unbelievably intricate maze had appeared on the screen.

"They only give you two minutes to get through *that*?" BJ said, seeing the countdown in a corner of the screen.

But to his astonishment, Darryl guided the figure

through the maze with twenty seconds to spare.

"Wow," he murmured as congratulations appeared on the screen.

There was quite a long pause; then a game list appeared. Darryl clicked on StarMaster 3.

"Skip the rules," BJ said. "I'll just watch."

Darryl answered the question "Want to play?" and learned that his opponent was called LabRat. After Darryl identified himself as MDK, a map of the universe appeared.

"It looks like the beginning of *Star Voyager*," BJ said. "That's my favorite movie of all time."

"Same here," said Darryl.

"Is Captain Geomopolis in this game?"

"Nah. What you have to do is . . . first you have to find out where the Controllers and the Individualists are."

"The what?"

Darryl explained as he played, and before long BJ was totally absorbed. Darryl's dexterity in steering his ships out of trouble was as remarkable as his knack for locating star gates, but what left BJ agog was his ability to recruit the Individualists by answering their questions. He'd never seen anything like it in his life.

"How old are you?"

"Twelve."

Same as him. He turned to ask Boris if his sister was as good as this.

Boris wasn't there. BJ looked under the beds. Under the one near the window was a battered suitcase covered with National Park stickers. Under the other there were only a couple of dust balls.

"Where the heck did he go?"

The desk chair squeaked as Darryl swiveled around. His eyes went straight to the tree out the open window.

"Think he climbed out?" BJ said, going over there.

There was no sign of Boris in the madrona tree. When he turned back, Darryl's face was as white as the pillowcases on the beds.

"What's wrong?"

Darryl's eyes were fixed on the night table. The only things on it were a lamp, the library book BJ had left last week, and a paperback called *The Expanding Universe*. The GameMaster was gone.

4

"**H**ere he comes now," Ms. Grimsley said as BJ rounded the curve of the lower staircase.

"Sugar pie," said his mother, "I've been waiting half an hour."

BJ said nothing as he joined the two women—one fat and chocolate colored, the other pale and stick thin—on the Oriental rug under the chandelier. Through an archway he could see kids eating breakfast in the dining room.

"What's the matter?" Mrs. Walker said.

BJ shrugged.

"What took you so long?"

"I was talking to this kid, Darryl," he mumbled. The truth was, Darryl's brilliance had shaken him.

"Were you really?" said Ms. Grimsley. "He hasn't said boo in eight days. Not even the counselor could get a word out of him. What were you talking about?"

"Nothing. He was playing this game, StarMaster 3."

"Well, I'm glad to hear that. Maybe he's coming around."

"Coming around from what?" BJ asked.

"He's been in shock. He lost his entire family in a fire."

"No!" Mrs. Walker cried.

"I'm afraid so. It was over on Bainbridge Island."

"Good lord, I saw something about that in the paper," Mrs. Walker said. "A family reunion, wasn't it?"

"His grandmother's birthday, I believe. The house went up in flames in the middle of the night. Nobody got out alive."

"Nobody?" BJ gasped. "How about Darryl?"

"He was sleeping in a tree house in the backyard. He lost his parents and his brother and his grand-parents. An aunt and uncle and cousin, too. We've been running a search for other family members, but so far we've come up blank."

"Can he come over for dinner, Ma?" BJ said, his jealousy turned to sympathy.

"Well, sweetie, that's a kind thought, but I'm not sure . . . "

"Are the kids prisoners here, Ms. Grimsley?" BJ asked.

"Prisoners? Not at all. But Darryl's been traumatized. He's barely eaten. He's fine, physically, according to the doctor, but he's in denial about the whole episode. What we do in these situations is we wait for the child to work himself out of it a bit before trying to place him."

"Bet you ten bucks he'd eat Ma's cooking."

"BJ," Mrs. Walker said, smiling in spite of herself.

"You'll like him, Ma. He's smarter than me."

"That I doubt."

"No, you will."

"I mean I doubt he's smarter than you. BJ's been top of his class the last two years."

Though Ms. Grimsley's mouth wasn't made for smiling, it did its best. "Good for you, young man. And I appreciate your taking an interest in Darryl. But at this point I think it would be best if he stayed put. He hasn't even cried yet. It's all still bottled up inside him."

"Poor guy," BJ said. "First his family, now his GameMaster."

"What do you mean? The GameMasters are bolted down."

"Not the laptop—his. That Boris guy grabbed it and took off out the window."

"*What!*"

"Who's Boris?" Mrs. Walker said.

Ms. Grimsley's natural frown was back. "Boris Rizniak. He showed up here a few weeks ago and we tried to place him—then he disappeared. He claims he's looking for his sister, but he's a dreadful liar. And a troublemaker. He must have had a rough upbringing—he has some ugly scars on his back—so when he showed up again yesterday, hungry and tired, I didn't have the heart not to take him in. But stealing! Next time it's juvenile detention."

Boris seemed to be in plenty of hot water already, so BJ didn't mention the cigarettes, which had also disappeared, or the switchblade in his pocket.

"Where's this Darryl from?" Mrs. Walker asked. "Bainbridge Island?"

"No, that's where his grandparents lived," Ms. Grimsley said. "He's from here in Seattle, just over on First Hill. A small house, mostly mortgaged. The parents didn't have any money to speak of. Very outdoorsy, apparently. They led hiking parties in the mountains."

"Sounds as if he might be able to use a little home cooking."

"Well, you may be right," said Ms. Grimsley. "But—"

"Great, Ms. Grimsley," BJ said, grabbing the old videos off the hall table. "We'll come back after we finish our rounds."

## 5

**D**arryl sat slumped on one of the beds. He hadn't felt much of anything over the past week, but now that the broad-shouldered black boy in the baggy jeans had left, he was feeling a little lonely.

Eventually a scuffling noise drew his eyes to the window. A squirrel was climbing up the madrona tree, circling the trunk like a stripe on a barber's pole. The same tree the other boy had climbed down with the GameMaster that had been given to him by . . .

It was as if he'd sucked in the vapor from a hunk of dry ice and quick-frozen his lungs. A woman's kindly voice rang in his head—*The only trouble with him is his brains. Super-smart people always think too much about things*—and his windpipe seemed to constrict so he could barely get a breath. Raking the room, his eyes fixed on the laptop.

For the third time he moved to the desk chair and hit a key. The colorful word MondoGameMaster comforted him.

He made it through the maze, and when the game list appeared, he again clicked on StarMaster 3. This time his opponent was called NABATW—which seemed strangely familiar, though he couldn't think why. Whoever it was, NABATW adapted to his moves even faster than HighFlier or LabRat, and in spite of having no distractions, he suffered a humbling defeat, his loyal troops all either killed or captured.

Annoyingly, a new maze popped up instead of the game list. But he negotiated it and quickly reintroduced himself to the mysterious NABATW. So began the most hard-fought struggle of his whole GameMaster career. The battle for the universe raged for nearly two hours until at last, partly by luck, partly by a skillful flanking maneuver, Darryl and his rebel troops forced the Controllers into surrender.

No maze popped up now: just a map of the universe, the setting for a third StarMaster 3 game. The deciding match was as grueling as the last one. NABATW was nothing like the preprogrammed opponent he was used to. Every time he devised a new strategy for securing wormholes and star gates, NABATW absorbed it, so if he tried it again, the Controllers were ready. The tide of the war kept shifting until, after two and a half hours, he and his Individualist legions were cornered near the Crab nebula. As the Controllers closed in, Darryl shot off a desperation vortex ray from his lead ship. It missed its target—the Controllers' command module—but triggered the explosion of another supernova behind it. Darryl just had time to put up his defensive shield while the debris from the monster star explosion completely annihilated the enemy.

Lucky as it was, he basked in his victory, grinning at the bosky-green universe. Then the screen went black and dark-red letters bled onto it, forming the name of a game he'd never heard of. It remained there alone, the only choice—DeathMaster—till it was replaced by the image of a face: a hairless, skull-like face with milky eyes and skin as wrinkled as an old paper bag. The face was so ancient, you couldn't tell if it was a man's or a woman's.

Slowly the face faded away, and the screen filled with words.

Suddenly, instead of playing a game, Darryl was reading a science text. *To understand the nature of matter, we must have a theory that accounts for both the qualitative and quantitative observations of matter and its behavior. . . .* After he'd read several screens full of information, a question popped up: *Lead has an atomic weight of 207.21 and a density of 11.4 g. per cc. What is the volume occupied by 2 gram-atoms of lead?* Applying what he'd just soaked up, he made his computation and typed in his answer: 36.4 cc. The ancient face reappeared, a slight smile on the fleshless lips.

The face vanished; more text appeared: about the

periodic table and molecular bonding and Faraday's laws of electrolysis. Darryl's head hurt, there was so much information, but as soon as another question popped up, his pulse quickened, even though there were no Individualists to win over, no wormholes to find. This question was about isotopes. Once he typed in his answer, the face reappeared, smiling again, but this time not quite so ancient, minus a couple of wrinkles, the eyes not quite so milky.

After six sections and six correctly answered questions, the jowls on the face didn't hang down so far, and you could tell it was a man. After ten sections and ten answers, the face got a facelift, and a few hairs popped out on the head. Just as the face was beginning to seem somehow familiar, a red light flashed in the left eyeball.

Next thing Darryl knew, someone was shaking him by the shoulder: the boy who'd saved him from the punk with the knife that morning. Darryl blinked at him, clueless as to how long he'd been sitting there frozen, sipping the air as if through a straw.

"Talk about lost in space. Too much StarMaster?"

Darryl grunted.

"We thought maybe you'd go for some home cooking. My mom's going to make her Swedish meatballs." The boy gave him a friendly punch. "You got a sweatshirt or something? It'll cool down later."

Darryl's eyes flicked to the bed nearer the window, but he looked away when BJ pulled the battered suitcase out from under it. Mrs. Grimsley had sent someone over to Darryl's house to get some of his clothes, and they'd brought them back in his mother's suitcase, which he'd immediately shoved out of sight.

"Cool, a MasterTech sweatshirt," the boy said. "Come on, Ma's waiting down in the car."

Five minutes later Darryl was sitting in the front seat of a Chevy Nova with a woman who introduced herself as Birdie Walker. She wasn't very birdlike. She took up half the front seat. But she radiated warmth, and as they drove out of Madrona, the shelter's neighborhood, into the Central District, Darryl felt himself unfreezing a little.

Mrs. Walker dropped the boys at home and went off to do some grocery shopping. Unlike Madrona, which had mostly big houses with views of Lake Washington, the Central District had mostly small houses with no views of the lake, and the Walkers' house was smaller than most, only one story. But it had a nice sky-blue paint job and a well-tended rock garden in front.

BJ led the way around to a backyard with a picnic table and a shiny red grill. The back door, which had one of those pet flaps in the bottom, led to a small storage-laundry room. On one side was a washer and dryer and ironing board; on the other, a stack of boxes, a bicycle with a basket on the front, and the biggest litter box Darryl had ever seen. As soon as they stepped from there into the kitchen, they were surrounded by half a dozen meowing cats.

"Hey, guys," BJ said.

He pulled a big bottle of Pepsi out of the fridge and filled a couple of tall plastic glasses. When he put the bottle away, Darryl noticed a placard held to the fridge door by magnets: *Knowledge is the ship to the Hesperides.*

"What's Hesperides?" he asked, unused to being stumped.

"It's an island where they grow apples made of gold. It's in the Sunday book."

"The what?"

"This book we read out of on Sunday instead of going to church. It's all about myths and religions of the world."

After scattering some cat treats on the kitchen floor, BJ showed Darryl the rest of the house: a hallway, a living room with a TV and VCR, and his mother's bedroom.

"Where do you sleep?" Darryl asked.

There were two doors in the hallway: one to a coat closet, one with another placard on it: *Knowledge is the stairway to Sirius.* But the stairway that was revealed when BJ opened the door didn't lead to any star; it led down to a spartan basement furnished with a bunk bed, a desk with a computer on it, a couple of hardback chairs, a shelf full of books, and a refrigerator. The refrigerator wasn't plugged in: It was BJ's closet. There was a small bathroom in the corner, and a small window up near the ceiling. Under the window was a poster of the Seattle Sonics' point guard. The wall over the desk was plastered with newspaper articles about Keith Masterly.

"I have this over *my* desk," Darryl cried, pointing at a cover of *Newsweek* with Keith Masterly's caricature on it.

"Really?" said BJ. "Hey, you're smart. What's that mean?" He pointed to the caption, *YouthMaster*, under Masterly's name. "Is it because he sells games to kids, or because he was so young when he started, or because he still looks so young?"

"Maybe all three?"

BJ pulled the switchblade from his pocket and stuck it in his desk drawer. "I still can't believe that weasel copped your GameMaster."

"Me either. Have you got one?"

"I'm saving up. But check this out."

BJ sat down and flicked on his computer. It was a dinosaur, a plodding old desktop, but it finally booted up. BJ clicked on an icon—at least he had a MasterTech mousepad—and a castle, familiar and forbidding, materialized on the screen. Flying from the tallest turret was a pennant with CastleMaster written on it.

"Pirated?" Darryl said, pulling up the other chair.

"Yeah. You've played, right?"

"Uh-huh."

"Want to go first?"

"Sure."

CastleMaster was the first game Keith Masterly had invented. It was far simpler than StarMaster or MasterTrek, but it was classic MasterTech in that it rewarded intelligence even more than eye-hand coordination. By answering brainteaser after brainteaser, Darryl gained access to the castle and evaded both of the evil duke's bodyguards—Feros the Barbarian and Quadros the Four-Headed Pit Bull. He proceeded to rescue the prisoners from the dungeon, lock up the evil duke in their place, and liberate the treasure the duke had amassed by overtaxing the poor.

"Jeez, I thought I was hot when I got up to Quadros in one turn," BJ said as Darryl led a parade of grateful prisoners, arms heaped with treasure, back over the drawbridge. "I never saw anything like that."

"Luck," Darryl said. "Your turn."

BJ got the first riddle (Q: When do elephants have eight feet? A: When there are two of them) but didn't

solve the math problem in time and so never crossed the moat.

"I usually do better than that," he muttered.

While they played, the ceiling creaked above them, and before long Mrs. Walker called them up to dinner. Darryl's family had been extremely fit, and when he sat down at the Walkers' kitchen table, the sight of Mrs. Walker's flabby arms and multiple chins didn't restore his missing appetite. But to be polite he sampled one of the Swedish meatballs.

"It's delicious, Mrs. Walker."

"Why, thank you, honey. What's the food like at that shelter?"

"I'm not really sure."

"Judging by that Ms. Grimsley, it can't be much. What's the matter with you, BJ? Were you snacking?"

BJ shook his head. He'd picked his fork up but put it back down without eating.

"You're not hungry?"

BJ shrugged.

"That's not like you, sugar pie. What is it?"

"Is Swedish meatballs brain food, Ma?"

"Brain food? What do you want with brain food, smart as you are?"

"I'm not smart."

"Of course you are! You're top of your class."

"Compared to Darryl, I'm a birdbrain."

"That's not true," Darryl said. "I've just had more practice."

"You should see him on CastleMaster, Ma," BJ said plaintively. "He don't miss."

"He *what?*"

"He doesn't miss. He's from another planet."

Mrs. Walker jiggled with amusement.

"What's so funny?" said BJ, scowling.

"I'm just tickled you found somebody to challenge you. BJ!"

"What?"

"I saw that."

"But Aristotle's hungry." He'd slipped a bit of meatball under the table to one of the cats.

"They have their own food. If you're not going to eat yours, I'll save it for leftovers."

She reached out for his plate, but instead of handing it over, BJ started eating. So did Darryl. Mrs. Walker was so kind and cheerful, he'd already stopped noticing how fat she was.

With every bite he took, Darryl grew hungrier, as if the meatballs were reminding his stomach what it was for. He had seconds, then thirds, and still had room for a bowl of ice cream.

The only time the cheerful expression deserted Mrs.

Walker's face during the meal was when BJ asked if they could catch the end of the Mariners game. "You were playing that computer game before dinner," she said. "After dinner you're doing some reading. That book on the Lewis and Clark Expedition."

"But what about Darryl?"

"You can read aloud to each other while I do the dishes. Then I'll drive him back to the shelter."

"Can't he sleep over, Ma?"

"I'd have thought you'd want to get rid of him, seeing as he makes you feel so stupid."

"Yeah, well, I was thinking about what you said. It's like those old heroes in the Sunday book. They only do the cool stuff when they get challenged. Like Hercules cleaning out those stables."

The smile crept back onto Mrs. Walker's face, and she relented on the baseball game, saying they could watch a few innings.

6

**B**ut the game was such a blowout—the M's were getting pulverized by the Angels—that BJ soon clicked the TV off in disgust and introduced Darryl to the cats, who had joined them on the living-room sofa: Galileo, Booker T, Aristotle, FDR, Gwendolyn—"named after some poet lady"—and the runt, Confucius.

"What about you?" Darryl said, scratching Booker T's neck. "What's BJ stand for?"

"Bawana Jamal."

"Is that African or something?"

"I guess. My dad gave it to me."

After a pause Darryl said, "Where is your dad?"

BJ didn't answer right off. His father wasn't his favorite subject. But seeing as Darryl had lost his whole family, BJ got the wedding photo down from the bookshelf. "Is that your mom?" Darryl whispered, looking at a slim, smiling woman standing on church steps beside a handsome, athletic man.

"Yeah."

"And that's . . . ?"

"Uh-huh."

Darryl pointed at the palm trees flanking the church steps. "It's not Seattle."

"San Diego. My dad got drafted by the Chargers."

BJ explained how his father had been a star line-backer at UW—the University of Washington—which was where he'd met and married his mother. The San Diego Chargers had picked him in the eighth round of the NFL draft, but he'd torn up his knee in training camp, and instead of following his bride's advice and giving up football for grad school, he'd had surgery and done intensive physical therapy and tried out for the team again the next summer.

"He still got cut. But even then he didn't give up." BJ noticed that Darryl's eyelids were drooping. "You bored with this?"

"No, no. I'm sorry."

"Mom's not big on talking about it, but I guess they spent the next three years traveling around in a trailer. Dad kept trying out for one team after another. You know, as a walk-on. Finally the Cards gave him a shot. But in the third exhibition game he tore up the same knee, worse than the first time. A few weeks later he had a head-on with an eighteen wheeler. That was three months before I was born. They found all these pills in his stomach—painkillers. So, anyway, you can see why Mom's not too big on sports. Darryl?"

Incredibly, Darryl's head had fallen back against the sofa, eyes closed. The guy asked about his father, something he never talked about, then fell asleep in the middle of his story!

But it was hard to stay angry at him, considering what he'd been through. Some of BJ's friends were suspicious of white people, but there was something about Darryl he really liked. When his mother came in with her decaf, he said:

"Why don't you call Grimface and see if he can spend the weekend?"

Mrs. Walker took a sip of coffee to hide her smile over "Grimface."

"I don't see why not." She went back to the kitchen and returned after a couple minutes. "I told her he'd eaten a big dinner and fallen sound asleep—so she said maybe home cooking *was* what he needed. She's going to pick him up at eight o'clock Monday morning."

"Great."

BJ dragged their groggy guest down to the basement and put him to bed in the bottom bunk. Darryl still hadn't appeared at noon the next day when BJ and his mother finished a chapter about the Mayans and their rain gods in the Sunday book.

"I guess maybe we better wake him," Mrs. Walker said, sliding the fat book back into its place of honor between the dictionary and the *Complete Shakespeare*. "Otherwise the poor boy'll be up all night."

It was a bright, sunny day, and after lunch—breakfast for Darryl—Mrs. Walker dropped them at Madison Beach, where the two boys spread their towels on the grassy slope above Lake Washington.

"Keith Masterly lives over there," Darryl said, pointing across the water.

"I've seen pictures of the house in magazines," BJ said. "It's awesome. It's got a helipad and everything. But they never say exactly where it is."

"Hunt's Point. Above the floating bridge."

"How do you know?"

Darryl didn't reply.

"How do you know, man?"

"I knew someone who worked for MasterTech," he said, just audibly.

"Wow. Cool."

But he could tell Darryl didn't want to talk about it—maybe it was someone in his family—so BJ dropped the subject.

When they swam out to the diving float, BJ got a little revenge for the whippings Darryl had given him at CastleMaster. After baking for a while, he lobbied for going off the high board—and Darryl went as pale as when he'd lost his GameMaster. So BJ got to show off his flip and his half gainer while Darryl stayed glued to the float.

Later they walked home up Madison. When they got to Cherry Street, a bunch of BJ's friends came swooping around the corner on skateboards.

"Yo, BJ," Big T said, dismounting. "What's happening, bro?"

"Not much," BJ said. "Where you been?"

Big T flipped his board up with his foot and grabbed it by the front truck. "Myrtle Edwards," he said.

BJ didn't have a board—if he'd gotten one, his mother would have taken an axe to it—and though Big T had lent him his number-two board a few times, he'd never gone as far as the Myrtle Edwards Trail, which ran north of the Seattle waterfront. To get there, you had to go through downtown, and if a friend of his mother's spotted him there, he would be cooked.

"Come on, we're all meeting at the DQ."

"Um, this is Darryl. Darryl, Big T."

Darryl stuck out his hand, but Big T shook it for barely a second, as if it was dirty or something.

"Coming, BJ?" Big T said.

"I got to be getting home."

"Later then."

With that Big T dropped his board in the street and took off.

"Did I do something wrong?" Darryl asked.

"Nah," BJ said, a little ashamed of his friend.

Back at home they played CastleMaster, Darryl once more hurdling every obstacle with awe-inspiring skill, and later Mrs. Walker took them to Capitol Hill Pizza. Darryl conked out on the ride home, so again BJ dragged him down to the basement and put him to bed in the bottom bunk. When he went back upstairs, his mother was in the laundry room dumping the contents of the litter box into a garbage bag.

"Sorry, Ma." Cleaning the litter box was one of his duties.

"That's all right, sugar pie, you have company." She poured new litter into the box. "That sure is one sleep-deprived boy."

"I think he likes it here." After a moment he added: "I was thinking."

"Well. I'm glad to hear that."

"I was thinking he should stay with us."

"Darryl?"

"Like you could adopt him or something. He'd make a great brother, even if he is white."

Mrs. Walker tied up the bag of old litter securely and dumped it in the trash.

"Don't you like him, Ma?"

"I like him a lot."

"He's a genius, I'm sure of it. He'd be a good influence on me. And he lived just over on First Hill. He could still go to his old school from here—or he could transfer to Garfield. Though he's smarter than any of our teachers."

"I'm afraid I can't afford another mouth to feed, honey."

"Ronnie Johnson's got an aunt in Everett who takes in kids and gets money from the government. I'll bet you could get some, too."

"I wouldn't be so sure about that."

"Ask Mr. Botts. I bet he knows." Clara Botts, who worked with her at the library, had a lawyer husband.

"You only just met Darryl, sugar pie," Mrs. Walker said, leading the way into the kitchen. "How about some chocolate milk?"

"You don't need to know somebody for a long time to *know* them. You told me you knew you wanted to marry Dad after one date."

"That's a little different."

"I just feel for the guy."

Mrs. Walker took his hand and gave it a squeeze.

## 7

"Time to get up, Darryl, honey. It's eight o'clock."

Swimming up out of a deep sleep, Darryl placed the voice as Mrs. Walker's. Springs squeaked overhead: BJ rolling over in the bunk above. Once again he'd mysteriously ended up in the bottom bunk in the basement.

Darryl had zero desire to get up. It was so much nicer here, with BJ up above him, than in the third-floor room at the shelter, with the spider overhead. BJ made him feel safe. Maybe it was his voice, which was already deep and grown-up, or the way he'd disarmed that Boris guy so easily. Or his size. They were the same age, but BJ must have had three inches and a good twenty-five pounds on him.

"Up and at 'em, honey," Mrs. Walker called again.

He didn't want to disobey her. She'd given him a new toothbrush and paid for his two slices of pepperoni pizza. He tossed back the blanket, swung his feet down to the cool basement floor, put on his shoes, brushed his teeth, and started up the stairs.

He paused halfway up. "See you soon?"

BJ let out an unintelligible groan.

"You slept in your clothes again, didn't you?" Mrs. Walker said when Darryl walked into the kitchen. "Let me run an iron over that shirt. I'm not sending you back worse than I picked you up."

"But I'm not worse," he said, undoing his shirt buttons. "I left the toothbrush down there in case I come back. Is that okay?"

"Of course it is, honey. Now sit down and have a bowl of cereal."

As he ate his raisin bran, one of the cats jumped up onto his lap and licked his bare stomach, just above his belly button, with his scratchy tongue.

"Morning, Galileo," he said, stroking the cat's fur with his free hand.

After eating, he set Galileo on the floor and rinsed the bowl and spoon and stuck them into the dishwasher. Soon Mrs. Walker came in from the back room with his shirt. It didn't have a wrinkle and felt cozily warm.

"Well, look what the cats dragged in," Mrs. Walker said as BJ shuffled into the kitchen. "Morning, sugar pie."

"Morning," BJ mumbled. His hair was mushed down on one side from his pillow.

"You should feel honored, Darryl. He never gets up this early in the summer."

"Grimface here?" BJ asked, sitting down at the kitchen table.

"Maybe she forgot about me," Darryl said hopefully.

But the words were barely out of his mouth when the doorbell rang. Neither of the boys moved, so Mrs. Walker went. Soon she ushered the guest into the kitchen.

"Well, Darryl, you're looking better, I must say," Ms. Grimsley said. "Mrs. Walker's cooking must have agreed with you."

"I like it here, Ms. Grimsley," Darryl said.

"We want to keep him," said BJ. "Don't we, Ma?"

"Well, it's a possibility," Mrs. Walker said.

"Really?" Ms. Grimsley said, looking around her. "Would Mr. Walker agree with you?"

"The only Mr. Walker's me," said BJ.

"I see," Ms. Grimsley said, not very optimistically.

"May I offer you a cup of coffee?" Ms. Walker said.

"Thank you, but I'm afraid Darryl and I have to be on our way."

"He can come visit us, right?" BJ asked. "While we're doing the application stuff?"

"The shelter's not a jail."

"And I can visit there?"

"Of course."

The four of them walked out to the curb, where Ms. Grimsley had parked her little Toyota.

"We'll come see you when I get off work, honey child," Mrs. Walker said, giving Darryl a hug.

"Later, bro," BJ said, clasping his hand.

Darryl climbed in the front seat. He kept his eyes on BJ and his mother out the window as the car slowly pulled away.

"Your house isn't far from here," Ms. Grimsley said after making a left. "Would you like to swing by?"

"No, thank you."

"Mrs. Walker seems like a very nice woman," Ms. Grimsley said, turning onto Madison.

"She is."

"BJ seems like a nice boy, too."

Darryl could tell Ms. Grimsley was trying to be kind, but the ripples of loneliness going through him put him back in his untalky mood, so they were soon driving along in silence. At the brow of the hill Ms. Grimsley pulled the driver's side sun visor down. Darryl just shut his eyes against the morning sun and tried to time travel back an hour, to the bottom bunk in the basement. He kept his eyes shut tight when the car turned left, and when it turned right, and even when the tires crunched on the shelter's gravel driveway.

"Now what's that old wreck doing there?" Ms. Grimsley said, clucking her tongue.

As the car came to a stop, Darryl cracked his eyes. Parked up ahead on the gravel circle was a dented old VW van: ready for the junkyard, by the look of it.

8

When the Nova pulled into the little driveway, BJ, who'd been waiting on the front step since getting home from the basketball courts at Garfield, strode over and opened the passenger-side door.

"Ready, Mom?"

"Can't I change my clothes, sugar pie?" Mrs. Walker said.

"But you look great! And I was thinking, they probably eat early there. If we get there during dinner, they might not let us see Dare."

Climbing in and out of the car wasn't Mrs. Walker's favorite pastime, so she told him to hop in.

"Bring home a video?" he asked, patting his mother's bulging book bag.

"Just papers. I did a little research on adoption at work."

"What did you find out?"

"Well, I found out it helps if you have assets."

"Dare and I could get part-time jobs or something."

She smiled. "I wouldn't get my hopes up, sweetie— but if it does work out somehow, there's something you should be prepared for."

"People giving us weird looks because he's white?"

"No. Not being the smartest kid on the block any-more."

BJ laughed.

Soon they were crunching up the Masterly Children's Shelter's gravel drive, and before Mrs. Walker could set the emergency brake, BJ was out of the car and bounding onto the wide front porch. A redheaded girl was sitting in one of the wicker chairs, her nose in a comic book.

"When do you guys eat?" BJ asked.

"Six-thirty," she said, barely looking up. "But you gotta be checked in."

"I just want to see my friend. You know Darryl?"

"Darryl?" she said, looking up.

"Darryl Kirby."

"Skinny guy with messy blond hair?"

"Yeah."

"Good luck."

"Why?"

She just went back to the comic. The porch creaked as Mrs. Walker stepped up onto it. BJ held the door for his mother and followed her inside.

"That girl thinks we won't get to see Darryl," he murmured.

"Nonsense," said Mrs. Walker.

She walked up to the office door and knocked.

Ms. Grimsley looked startled when she opened it.

"Didn't you get my message, Mrs. Walker?"

"What message?"

"The one I left on your machine."

"What did you say?"

"That Darryl's been placed."

"*Placed?* With foster parents?"

"Yes."

"You can't mean it!"

"It *was* rather quick. Um, please, won't you come on in and sit down?"

Mrs. Walker stepped into the office and sat on the couch, but BJ remained in the doorway. "Where is he?" he asked accusingly.

"BJ, really," said Mrs. Walker. "But where is Darryl, Ms. Grimsley?"

Ms. Grimsley sat down at her desk and, removing her glasses, pressed the bridge of her nose between two bony fingers. "I'm afraid that's classified."

A rare frown appeared on Mrs. Walker's face. "What do you mean, 'classified'?"

"It's an unusual situation, Mrs. Walker. But trust me, Darryl's in good hands."

"We want to see him!" BJ cried.

"We were seriously thinking about filing for adoption," said Mrs. Walker. "Where is he?"

"I really am afraid I can't tell you," Ms. Grimsley said. "But perhaps Darryl will get in touch with you."

"Perhaps!" BJ cried. "What do you mean, 'perhaps'?"

Instead of scolding him for his abruptness, Mrs. Walker echoed his words: "What do you mean, 'perhaps'?"

The phone on Ms. Grimsley's desk rang.

"Yes, hello? Ah, certainly—would you give me a moment, please?" She covered the receiver. "I'm sorry, do you think you could wait out in the hall?"

Mrs. Walker heaved herself up with a humph and closed the door behind her as she left. By that time BJ was already out the front door.

"Where'd Darryl go?" he asked the redhead.

"Search me."

"When did he leave?"

"This morning."

"Who with?"

"Some foster parents, probably. That's what they do here, you know—pawn you off on foster parents." She smirked complacently. "Unless nobody wants you."

"You didn't see them?"

"The foster parents? Uh-uh. Or only from my window. It was early—I just got up."

"What'd they look like?"

"Who knows? They had on hats."

"What kind of car'd they have?"

"One of those old hippie cars."

"What do you mean?"

"One of those vans from like a million years ago, the seventies or something."

A bell rang.

"Grub," the girl said, popping up.

BJ followed her back inside and reported his findings to his mother. As a motley assortment of kids migrated through the front hall bound for the dining room, BJ interrogated each one about Darryl's departure. But only a couple had even laid eyes on Darryl—he hadn't eaten a single meal in the dining room—and no one added anything to the porch girl's information.

"Sorry about that, Mrs. Walker," Ms. Grimsley said, emerging from her office. "Now, is there anything else I can do for you?"

"Anything else! But you haven't done anything! We have no idea where Darryl is."

"I wish I could help you."

"Then why don't you?"

"I'm sorry. I'm afraid we're having our dinner."

"Let's go, Ma," BJ said angrily. "I'll bet there's a message from him on the machine."

But when they got home, the only message was from Ms. Grimsley, left hours ago, advising them cheerfully that Darryl had been placed with a lovely foster family.

## 9

**M**s. Grimsley hadn't been so cheerful when she'd pulled up behind the battered van that morning.

"I can't imagine what they're delivering," she said crossly, "but they should have gone around back. That thing looks as if it's about to fall to pieces."

Darryl followed her past the broken-down van and up the porch steps into the shelter. None of the children were down yet, but the woman in yellow was setting the dining-room table for breakfast.

"Who's that parked out front?" Ms. Grimsley asked.

"They're in your office, ma'am."

"You have your old room to yourself now, Darryl. I'll be ringing the breakfast bell shortly."

As Ms. Grimsley marched into her office, Darryl started up the front stairs. But after a few steps he heard an oddly familiar voice and stopped.

"You must be Ms. Grimsley."

"I am. May I ask if that's your van parked out front?"

"Mm. We were hoping you could help us. We're looking to adopt, you see. This is my wife, Angie."

"I'm sorry to disappoint you, but you can't just pick

up a child like a hamburger at a fast-food joint. We have procedures here at Masterly. Yes, Darryl?"

Darryl had crept back down and was standing in the office doorway. But he wasn't looking at Ms. Grimsley. He was gaping at a man in a fedora hat sitting on the couch beside a beautiful woman in a similar hat. Though shadowed by his hat's brim, the man's eyes gave off a mesmerizing glitter.

"How are you, young man?" he said.

Darryl couldn't find his tongue.

"Go on upstairs, Darryl," Ms. Grimsley said. "Breakfast'll be in a few minutes."

"Is Darryl one of your guests?" the man asked.

"You could say that."

The man stood up and strode toward the door. He wasn't that tall or powerfully built, and he was casually dressed in jeans and running shoes and a lightweight sports jacket, but he radiated such self-assurance that he seemed to fill the room with his presence. "It's a pleasure to meet you," he said, giving Darryl's hand a firm shake. "My name's . . . but you know that, don't you?"

Darryl nodded once more.

"You know this man?" said Ms. Grimsley. "Is he related to you, Darryl?"

Darryl shook his head.

"I think I'd like to be," the man said, laying a hand on Darryl's shoulder.

"I'm sorry, but that's not the way we operate, Mr. . . ."

"But Ms. Grimsley," Darryl said, finally finding his voice. "He's Keith Masterly."

The man removed his hat. "A very perspicacious young man you have here, Ms. Grimsley."

Ms. Grimsley was pale by nature, but now what little blood she had in her face drained out of it. She removed her glasses, blinked at the man, put her glasses back on.

"Mr. Masterly!" she gasped.

"And, as I said, my wife, Angie."

The beautiful woman rose from the couch and removed her hat, releasing a cascade of golden hair. Mr. Masterly looked remarkably young for forty-six—that, Darryl knew, was his current age—but his wife, his second, could have been his daughter. As Darryl knew from newspaper reports, she was only twenty-two.

"Nice meeting you," Mrs. Masterly purred.

"Mr. Masterly!" Ms. Grimsley said, repeating herself. "But . . . but what . . . what are you . . . ?"

"What am I doing here? As I said, we're interested in adopting. We thought perhaps you could help us."

"Help you?" Ms. Grimsley echoed, as if she was losing her grip on the English language.

"Is Darryl available, by any chance? He strikes me as just what we had in mind. How old are you, Darryl—about twelve?"

Darryl nodded, staring unblinkingly at the face he knew so well from newspapers and magazines and TV interviews. And also, he now realized, from the DeathMaster game on the MondoGameMaster. If the face had continued to grow younger, it would have become Keith Masterly's.

"Twelve's ideal," Mr. Masterly said. "Of course, Darryl might not be interested in *us*, but if he is, we'd certainly be interested in him. We've been wanting to adopt for some time, and last night I had a dream about it. It probably sounds silly to you, Ms. Grimsley, but I'm a big believer in dreams. That's where I get the ideas for most of my games. So first thing this morning we drove straight over here. Sorry about the jalopy, by the way. It keeps the press from hounding us."

"Naturally," Ms. Grimsley said hoarsely.

"Tell me, Darryl. What's your last name?"

Darryl cocked his head to one side. "Don't you know, Mr. Masterly?"

Now Mr. Masterly's face paled slightly. "How would I know your name?"

"Aunt Ellie," he said, just audibly.

"His whole family died in a fire," Ms. Grimsley said

quietly, "including his aunt. I believe she worked for your company."

Mr. Masterly smiled at Darryl. "So you didn't buy my dream story, eh? You are a perspicacious boy—Darryl Kirby."

Darryl couldn't help grinning. Not only did Keith Masterly know his name, he considered him smart! He was almost positive that was the meaning of "perspicacious."

"I'm sure it's hard to have to think about such things at a time like this, Darryl," Mr. Masterly went on gently. "But we really would be delighted if you'd give us a whirl. I think in time you might grow to like us. And, of course, if you don't, you can just say the word and we'll bring you back here."

"But you already have a son, sir," said Darryl. Keith Jr., now eighteen, a product of his first marriage.

"Didn't I read somewhere that your son's a gifted water-skier?" Ms. Grimsley said.

"Yes, he's a gifted water-skier," Mr. Masterly said. "Do you water-ski, Darryl?"

Darryl shook his head.

"Well, I'm sure Kit would love to teach you. I hope you'll like him." A beep sounded. Mr. Masterly checked his watch—or, rather, a small monitor he wore on his wrist, much like Captain Geomopolis's in *Star Voyager*.

"Unfortunately, I've got a board meeting at ten-thirty. I don't suppose we could wrap this up?"

"Wrap this up?" Ms. Grimsley said, turning into a human parrot.

"As you so justly put it, this isn't a fast-food joint. We don't want Darryl feeling like a quarter pounder with cheese."

Darryl laughed.

"Still, Ms. Grimsley, I was hoping you might make an exception in our case. But if you feel we need references, or a background check, I perfectly understand."

"References! Background check! How could you think such a thing, Mr. Masterly? Good gracious, I've never heard of anything so ridiculous in my life!"

"Then I guess that leaves it up to our young friend," Mr. Masterly said. "You were fond of your aunt, weren't you, Darryl?"

Darryl swallowed, nodding. "She got me my GameMaster," he said softly.

The thingamajig on Mr. Masterly's wrist beeped again. "Sorry to be in such a hurry. What do you say, Darryl? Want to give us a test drive?"

"It's very nice of you to ask me, Mr. Masterly. I mean, I really appreciate it a lot. But BJ and his mom want to adopt me."

"Now, Darryl," Ms. Grimsley said. "You should

know how unlikely it is that Mrs. Walker would ever be approved. She's a single, working parent. And by the look of the house, with very few assets."

"BJ's a friend?" said Mr. Masterly.

Darryl nodded.

"Does he water-ski?"

"I don't think so."

"Well, I guess Kit'll have two students then."

"But . . . how would he get over to Hunt's Point? Mrs. Walker works at the library, so she couldn't drive him."

"I wouldn't worry about that," Mr. Masterly said. "We can send a driver for him whenever you want."

"Could I go along? And sometimes could I spend the night at BJ's?"

"Darryl, really, you mustn't bargain with Mr. Masterly," Ms. Grimsley said.

"Shows he has a sound head on his shoulders," Mr. Masterly said. "I'm sure we can work things out to everyone's satisfaction." He led the way into the front hall. "Do you have luggage, Darryl?"

"Why don't you run up and get your bag?" Ms. Grimsley said.

Darryl shook his head.

"We'll take you shopping later," Mr. Masterly said.

Only when they were back out on the gravel driveway

did Darryl notice the chauffeur sitting behind the wheel of the van. He had on a dark-red uniform and cap.

"I hope you realize how lucky you are, Darryl," Ms. Grimsley said.

As if to confirm this, the chauffeur popped out of the van and slid open the side door, revealing an interior that was as plush and luxurious as the outside was decrepit: four leather bucket seats grouped around a shiny walnut table. Darryl followed Mrs. Masterly in and sat down.

"We were thinking maybe you wouldn't have had breakfast, Darryl," Mrs. Masterly said, smiling at a plate of pastries on the table. "Help yourself."

There was a napoleon, and a buttery thing shaped like a little boat, and a heart-shaped pastry with glazed apple slices, and a lemon tart with a dollop of whipped cream on it. The napoleon looked the best, but it was coated with powdered sugar, and Darryl didn't want to make a mess, so he chose the one with apples. It was the most delicious thing he'd ever tasted in his life.

## 10

# M

r. Masterly walked Ms. Grimsley back up onto the porch of the Masterly Children's Shelter and asked if she would be so good as to do him one small favor.

"If the press gets wind of our adopting Darryl, we'll be under siege. We won't have a moment's peace, and the poor boy's life will be turned upside down. And then there's the kidnaping issue. We had two close calls with Keith Jr. when he was younger. So I'd prefer to keep the whole thing quiet."

"I understand perfectly."

"I appreciate your discretion, Ms. Grimsley." He shook her skeletal hand. "And I also appreciate the job you've been doing here. When was the last time you had a raise?"

"Oh, but sir—"

"When was the last time you had a raise, Ms. Grimsley?"

"Let me see. Two years and four and a half months ago, I got a cost-of-living raise."

"High time for another. And thank you again."

Mr. Masterly strode down to the van and climbed in

the back. The chauffeur slid the door shut and went around to the driver's seat, which was divided from the back by a panel of smoky glass. To communicate with him, Mr. Masterly pressed a button on the gizmo on his wrist.

"Home, Frank," he said into it—and off they went.

The back of the van was so soundproof that Darryl couldn't even hear the crunch of the tires on the gravel.

"You liked the *chausson aux pommes*?" Mr. Masterly said.

Darryl nodded enthusiastically. Mr. Masterly pressed a button on his wrist again and spoke into it:

"We're on the way in, Jimmy. Fire up the copter for me."

Darryl's eyes widened. Fire up the copter!

"Do you have to fly to the board meeting, sir?"

Mr. Masterly pulled a green bottle of mineral water out of a mini fridge in the wall and took a swig.

"To tell you the truth, Darryl, I don't have a board meeting. I sometimes beep myself when people bore me. Ms. Grimsley's pleasant enough, but a bit tiresome—don't you think? Which reminds me." He pressed another button on his wrist gizmo. "Charles? KM here. Speak to the Foundation and see that a Ms. Grimsley at the shelter in Seattle has her salary doubled ASAP. Oh, and—Darryl, what kind of car does she drive?"

"It's a little Toyota. Pretty old."

"Charles, get her a new car, too, on my personal account. . . . Oh, a Mercedes. . . . Let's see, nothing too sporty, I shouldn't think. A sedan. Top of the line. Thanks."

Her salary doubled *and* a new Mercedes!

"So, tell me about school, Darryl," Mr. Masterly said. "You must get top grades."

As he described his middle school, Darryl looked back and forth between Mr. and Mrs. Masterly. Neither face had a single wrinkle, and yet somehow you could tell Mr. Masterly was middle-aged while Mrs. Masterly was barely an adult. She didn't say another word till they were halfway across the Evergreen Point floating bridge.

"Look!" she suddenly cried, pointing out the tinted window on the side of the van. "Barefoot!"

On the south side of the bridge a sleek powerboat with a dark-red hull was shooting along at the speed of the eastbound car traffic. The man at the helm was wearing a uniform identical to the chauffeur's; the skier, about twenty-five yards behind the boat, was kicking up an unusual amount of spray. He was young and very handsome—tan and surfer blond—and looking closer, Darryl saw that he had on no water skis at all. He was skiing on the soles of his feet!

"Is that your son?" Darryl said.

Mr. and Mrs. Masterly spoke at the same time, Mr. Masterly saying, "I'm afraid so," Mrs. Masterly saying "Isn't he something?"

"You're not big on sports, sir?" Darryl asked.

"I have nothing against them," Mr. Masterly said. "I exercise regularly myself. But they can be a gigantic waste of time—and time's the only thing of value in the world."

Darryl yawned—not because he was bored but because all of a sudden he felt as sleepy as on the way back from the pizza parlor last night. "I think you'll like BJ's mom," he said, leaning his head back against the buttery leather seat. "She thinks sports are a waste of time, too."

His eyelids drooped and he felt strangely light-headed, as if he was rising up out of himself like a ghost. He seemed to float straight up through the van's tinted sunroof, up into the cloudless sky, the van and ski boat down below getting smaller and smaller and smaller till they were nothing at all.

## 11

"**S**omething's not right, Ma," BJ said, ripping a fourth sheet of paper towel off the roll. "He should have called by now."

They were grilling baby back ribs in the backyard. Though the barbecue sauce tasted great, it seemed to end up everywhere: on BJ's chin, his fingers, even his cutoffs. Next to a cordless phone in the middle of the picnic table was a roll of paper towels.

"Maybe that new foster family of his is keeping him busy," said Mrs. Walker.

"Still. It's been a day and a half."

"Maybe they don't live in Seattle. Maybe the call's long distance."

"He'd find a way. I'm worried, Ma."

"But Ms. Grimsley wouldn't have let him go with a family that wouldn't treat him well. They check every-thing out."

"That's another thing. There's something weird about that message she left yesterday."

"What do you mean?"

BJ stood up and, grabbing one of his mother's hands,

tugged her out of her chair. He led the way into the kitchen and hit the playback button on the answering machine on the end of the kitchen counter.

"Listen, I saved it," he said as FDR leaped up onto the counter and started licking barbecue sauce off his fingers.

"Hello, Mrs. Walker, Dorothea Grimsley here. I just wanted you to know we've placed Darryl with a lovely family. To save you a trip over here. It's now, let's see, it's three P.M. on Monday. Hope you're having a good day."

"See what I mean?" BJ said after the ending beep.

"What's weird about it?"

"You can't tell?"

"You mean them placing Darryl so fast?"

"Well, that, too. But I'm talking about Grimface. Her voice."

"What about it?"

BJ hit the playback button again, and the message replayed.

"Don't you see? She sounds happy."

"So?"

"She's not a happy person, Ma."

"Mm, she is kind of like an undertaker without any caskets."

"Yeah. So why would she be happy all of a sudden

just because she found Darryl some foster parents?"

"Maybe that's what makes her happy—placing kids."

"You buy that? I think something's fishy."

"Wash your hands, sugar pie, and let's go finish dinner. There's nothing we can do but wait for him to call."

"I'm done with dinner."

His mother followed him into the living room and watched him collapse on the floor. "I brought home a couple of videos," she said.

He just lay there with Confucius on his chest and Gwendolyn on his belly.

"Uh-oh," she said. "You've gone catatonic."

That was pretty funny—*catatonic*—but even so, he didn't laugh. His mother sank down on the sofa and squeezed the toes of his right foot through his Nike.

"I know your feelings are hurt, sweetie, but I'm sure Darryl—"

"My feelings aren't hurt!" BJ cried, sitting up so abruptly that the two cats flew halfway to the TV set and scuttled out of the room. "I'm just worried."

"Well, I'm going to finish my dinner."

When his mother left, BJ flopped down on his back with a sigh. Soon Galileo came over and started licking barbecue sauce off his cheek. BJ waited till the cat was done; then he picked him up and held him close to his chest, stroking his fur.

"You wouldn't just take off and forget about us, would you, boy?" he murmured. For in fact his feelings *were* hurt. "You're a nice, loyal cat, aren't you? What's the point of worrying about Dare if he's not worrying about us, huh? Yeah, that's right. You're a good little cat, yeah, you are. . . ."

At first it looked like Mars in MasterTrek, but after rubbing the sleep out of his eyes and blinking a few times, Darryl saw that it was a glowing globe of rosy glass: a ceiling lamp. He stretched his arms out to his sides. The sheets were cool and crisp. He sat up a bit. He had on his underpants and T-shirt and was surrounded by pillows. Three, four—six pillows! He sat up a little more and peered out across a feather-light comforter at a room as big as the whole downstairs of his old house.

"Back among the living, I see."

His head jerked around. Off to his right were a table and two red-velvet armchairs, one occupied by a man whose face was lit by the glow from a laptop computer in his lap. Darryl jumped out of the other side of the bed and stood at attention.

"Mr. Masterly!"

"Hi, Darryl."

Was it possible Keith Masterly had really watched over him while he napped? "What . . . what time is it?"

"Noon."

It had been around ten o'clock when Darryl had dozed off in the decrepit van with the fancy interior. "I can't believe I took a nap in the morning. I'm really sorry. I hope you didn't have to carry me!"

"Don't worry about it."

Twice in two days he'd conked out in a car and needed to be carried!

"How are you feeling?" Mr. Masterly asked.

In fact, Darryl was famished, in spite of the pastry he'd eaten. "I'm kind of hungry, sir," he said.

"Small wonder. You haven't eaten in over twenty-four hours."

"But I just had that . . . *chausson aux pommes*."

Mr. Masterly smiled. "That was yesterday."

"Yesterday?"

"It's Tuesday."

"What? What happened to Monday?"

"You've been in a state of shock lately, running on adrenaline. It's not unusual to sleep that long, under the circumstances."

Darryl was stupefied. Once, when he'd had the flu, he'd slept twelve hours, but that was his record, at least since he was a baby. Over twenty-four hours didn't seem possible.

He looked around for a window. Across the room were some drawn curtains, but he felt embarrassed about parading around in his underwear in front of Mr. Masterly.

"Excuse me, sir, but do you know where my clothes are?"

"You might check in there," Mr. Masterly said, pointing at the doorless wall beyond Darryl.

"Where, sir?"

"There."

As Darryl stepped tentatively that way, a panel in the wall slid open, revealing a plushly carpeted dressing room, itself twice the size of the bedroom he used to share with his brother. He walked in. To his right was a gleaming, blue-tiled bathroom with a glassed-in shower and a Jacuzzi, to his left a mirror that showed how messy his hair was. As he stepped closer to it, combing with his fingers, the mirror parted, revealing a walk-in closet with dozens of shirts on hangers and a set of drawers and a shoe rack. The top drawer contained dozens of pairs of brand-new socks, every color, each with a small PL embroidered in dark-red thread. The second drawer was full of underpants: all white with the same dark-red PL on the waistband, all Darryl's size. The third drawer was for T-shirts, all colors, all his size, all with PL on the right sleeve. The shoe rack held the sort of jelly shoes you wear at the beach, again in a dozen colors, all his size.

When he pulled a shirt off its hanger, he discovered

it wasn't a shirt at all but a futuristic jumpsuit with a PL patch on the chest. He pulled out another, a dark-blue one, and put it on. He found a pair of matching shoes, put them on, and stepped backward. The mirrored doors closed. Staring back at him was a Darryl right out of *Star Voyager*.

In the bathroom he washed the sleep out of his eyes and brushed his teeth. Along with a toothbrush and toothpaste on a glass shelf over the sink was a selection of fancy soaps, bottles of mouthwash and eau de cologne, a stick of deodorant, a hairbrush and comb set, and a sleek-looking electric razor. He gave his hair a good brushing. Though he'd never shaved before, and had no whiskers to speak of, the razor looked so cool he would have tried it out if he hadn't been keeping one of the most important people in the world waiting.

"You look great," Mr. Masterly said as Darryl emerged from the dressing room.

"Thanks," he said, only now noticing that Mr. Masterly had on a similar futuristic outfit. "What's PL?"

"You'll see."

Darryl walked over to the far wall and pulled the curtains, but instead of the expected view of Lake Washington, there was a movie screen. Setting his laptop on the table, Mr. Masterly got up and brought Darryl a remote control. It had a GameMaster-like keyboard and a liquid crystal display panel at the top.

"Type in 'Movies.'"

Darryl did, and a list of categories scrolled across the LCD panel: Action, Western, Drama, Romance, Animated. He clicked on Action, and an alphabetized list of titles scrolled across the panel: *Abduction from the Castle of Terror, The Abominable Snowman Meets the Loch Ness Monster, Absolute Force*—every action movie he'd ever heard of and many, many more. He hit fast forward, speeding up the list, and clicked on one. Sure enough, the familiar opening credits of *Star Voyager* flashed onto the big screen.

"Unreal! It's twenty times bigger than a TV."

"You've got over twelve hundred movies to choose from," Mr. Masterly said.

"This is really my room?"

"Absolutely."

Delighted, Darryl realized he could watch the rest of the movie later and pressed the pause button. He looked around for a window, but his eyes settled on a nearby painting, a portrait of a woman with a mysterious smile.

"The *Mona Lisa*," he murmured.

"Perhaps you'd like something more modern? Try 'Art.'"

Darryl typed in "Art" on the remote. Another list of

categories appeared on the LCD panel: African, American, Australian Aboriginal, Chinese, Dutch, Egyptian, English, Flemish, French, German, Ancient Greek, Indian, Italian, Native American, Roman, Spanish . . . He clicked on American and soon replaced the *Mona Lisa* with colorful spatters of paint.

"Try 'Music,'" Mr. Masterly suggested.

Darryl typed in "Music" and, after weeding through a bunch of categories, selected a legendary Seattle grunge band.

"Not bad, huh?" said Mr. Masterly as a familiar rock anthem filled the room.

"Unbelievable!"

"Unfortunately, it can't produce food. How about some brunch?"

Darryl nodded enthusiastically, and Mr. Masterly pressed a button on his wrist device.

"Hedderly, will you please bring brunch for Darryl and me in room eight?"

His house was so big the rooms were numbered!

"How do we get some daylight, sir?" Darryl asked.

"You want more light?" Mr. Masterly turned a dimmer switch on the wall, and the rosy glow brightened.

"Aren't there any windows?" Darryl said.

"I'm afraid not. Security."

This made sense. Someone as rich and powerful as

Keith Masterly probably had enemies, or people who wanted to spy on him—and anyone could buzz by his house in a boat. The windows Darryl had seen in photos of the house must have been a false facade.

"Could I make a quick call, sir? BJ and his mom'll be worried about me. They'll never believe I slept a whole day!"

"Will you do me a favor first?" Mr. Masterly asked.

"Of course!"

"Listen to what I have to say."

Mr. Masterly sat back down in his red velvet chair and pointed at the one opposite. It was the most comfortable chair Darryl had ever sat in.

"I consider myself a pretty good judge of character, Darryl, and I've decided you're someone worth cultivating. You're part of a very small elite. Do you know what 'elite' means?"

"That you're snobby?"

"Not necessarily," Mr. Masterly said, smiling. "It means being part of a select group. I'm speaking in terms of intellect. I think you may be a genius, Darryl."

"Because I get straight As?"

"Let's just say it's an intuition. But the trouble is, young people with fine minds often don't get proper encouragement and guidance, and their natural intellect ends up going to waste."

"You must have had proper encouragement and guidance."

"I was one of the lucky ones. And I want you to be one of the lucky ones, too."

"You do?"

"Yes. I've decided to offer you a rare opportunity. In fact, the rarest in the world."

"What opportunity?"

"To change the course of human history."

Darryl waited for Mr. Masterly to smile again, to show he was kidding. But he didn't.

13

"**W**hat do you mean, sir?" Darryl asked a little breathlessly.

"I mean there's an opening at Paradise Lab, and I want to offer it to you."

"Paradise Lab? That's PL?"

Mr. Masterly nodded.

"What is it?"

"Do you know what a think tank is, Darryl?"

"A place where people sit around thinking?"

"More or less. Paradise is a kind of think tank. It's become the primary focus of my life. I've been scaling back at MasterTech, delegating some of my responsibilities. I still enjoy dreaming up the games, but the business side has become tedious. Whereas Paradise is never tedious."

"Where is it?"

"Right here in Washington State."

"Really? I never heard of it."

"It's top secret."

"Is it really a paradise?" Darryl asked, flattered to be let in on something top secret.

"Well, what do you think?"

"Excuse me?"

"This room is part of it."

"You mean it's in your house?"

Mr. Masterly shook his head. "We stopped by the house yesterday, then flew here last night."

"While I was asleep?" Darryl said, more flabbergasted by the moment.

"Do you like it?"

"It's great, but . . . you mean we're not on the lake?"

"We're in Paradise Lab."

"You mean . . . but where are we?"

"In Washington State, as I said. Have you ever thought about what paradise really is, Darryl?"

It was very hard to think about anything when he was feeling so disoriented. They weren't in the house on Hunt's Point; they were somewhere they'd had to fly to. In the copter? Mr. Masterly clearly wasn't going to get any more specific than "Washington State," seeing as it was top secret.

"Paradise would be a place where you're happy," Darryl said.

"Exactly. But what's happiness? The absence of unhappiness, perhaps? That's the conclusion I've come to. Do you know what the root of unhappiness is?"

"I'm not sure."

"The root of unhappiness is time."

Mr. Masterly's watch gizmo beeped. He went to the door and returned wheeling a little trolley, which he parked by the table between their chairs. The biggest thing on it was a silver dome with a handle formed of the letters PL. There was also a silver coffee pot, a gold-rimmed cup and saucer, two silver forks, linen napkins with a PL monogram, and two glasses of orange juice with small paper cups beside them.

"I hope you like eggs Benedict," Mr. Masterly said, releasing a puff of steam as he lifted the dome.

There, on a gold-rimmed plate, were twin mounds of poached egg and Canadian bacon perched on English muffins. Darryl had never had eggs Benedict, but they certainly smelled good.

"They're all yours," Mr. Masterly said.

"What about you?"

"I have to watch my weight."

Mr. Masterly plucked a dark-blue pill out of the little paper cup and took it with his juice. Darryl pulled a pale-blue pill out of the other paper cup.

"Our MasterPills," Mr. Masterly said. "They give you all the vitamins and minerals you need, plus they stimulate the brain cells. That one's designed specially for young people. Try it."

Darryl swallowed the pill with a swig of orange

juice. "Wow, fresh squeezed!" He tried the eggs. "These are great!"

He tried not to wolf down his brunch, but it was so good, it was hard not to.

"You were saying something about time, Mr. Masterly?" he said when his plate was clean.

Mr. Masterly poured himself a cup of coffee. "If you had to describe life as we know it in a word, Darryl, what would that word be?"

Darryl suspected life as he knew it, and as most people knew it, was pretty different from life as Keith Masterly knew it. "I'm not sure, sir."

"I suppose it would be expecting a lot for someone your age to have a *Weltanschauung*."

"A what?"

"An overview of the world. Even for someone who's lost his family." Mr. Masterly's wrist buzzed again. "Unfortunately, time is still my master. We'll have to continue this little talk later—if you're interested."

"Oh, yes!" Darryl said, afraid the buzz meant that he was boring the great man as Ms. Grimsley had.

"You accept my offer then?"

"Well, it sounds fantastic, sir. But . . ."

"But you have doubts. I understand. A pity, though."

"I didn't mean no! I only meant I wasn't sure."

"The trouble is," Mr. Masterly said, standing up,

"there are several others in line for the spot."

"For being adopted?"

"In a manner of speaking."

"What would I do there? I mean, here."

"Learn. And apply what you learn to unlocking the mysteries of the universe. For example, have you ever wanted to communicate with someone who's dead?"

As Darryl stared at it, the rosy globe lamp above Mr. Masterly's head turned fiery red. But instead of feeling hot, Darryl started to shiver.

"Darryl? Are you all right?"

"Isn't communicating with the dead impossible?" he said, barely above a whisper.

Mr. Masterly picked up the remote and pressed a button. The painting changed from loose, colorful splatters to a detailed still life of apples and peaches with a dead rabbit hanging on the wall in the background. "Fifty years ago people would have said doing that was impossible. If you believe something's impossible, it is. Open your mind, and the possibilities are infinite."

But the thought of talking with the dead was as painful as it was intriguing, and Darryl's mind veered away. "What about BJ?" he said. "Could we still learn to water-ski?"

"Not if you decide to stay here, I'm afraid. But if you prefer to water-ski the summer away, you certainly may."

"Is Paradise Lab in session now?"

"Paradise is always in session."

"No vacations?"

"Depends how you look at it. You might say it's all vacation, since being genuinely engaged in something is the only true source of pleasure in life. And at Paradise you're always engaged."

"Are there other kids here?"

"That's all there are, except for a small staff. Would you like a tour?"

His shivering abated, Darryl wiped his mouth with his PL napkin and followed Mr. Masterly out the door into a corridor with the same thick carpeting and gentle rosy lighting as the bedroom. Between Darryl's door, numbered 8, and the next, numbered 7, was a glassed-in trophy case. The figurines on the trophies looked like ordinary girls and boys, and Darryl soon got a glimpse through a doorway of the models, sitting around an oddly shaped table in a sumptuous dining hall. There were six kids: four boys and two girls. They all looked cheerful except the youngest-looking one, a girl about his age who seemed strangely familiar. She had curly blond hair, and her eyes looked sad—though this might just have been because they were magnified by thick glasses.

"They're just starting lunch," Mr. Masterly said,

leading Darryl past the doorway.

"Is the girl with curly hair from Seattle?" he asked.

"Nina? No, she's not."

"Huh."

At the end of the corridor Mr. Masterly pressed a button and an elevator opened. He stepped inside.

"Coming?"

Darryl hated elevators. He had ever since his cousin Barry's sixteenth birthday up in the Space Needle. The Space Needle's elevators were like capsules, and after squeezing into one behind his brother and Uncle Frank, he'd found himself pressed up against a door that was almost all window. As the elevator whooshed upward, seemingly through open space, people oohed and aahed at the expanding view of the city. But Darryl fainted. If the elevator hadn't been packed, he would have sunk onto the floor in a heap. As it was, he slumped back against his brother, who gave him a sharp jab and hissed, "What's your problem, wuss?"

"I'm not going to bite you, Darryl," Mr. Masterly said.

Darryl took a deep breath and stepped in. It didn't bother him at all: he felt pleasantly numb. Moreover, it was a pretty unscary elevator. There were no windows, and only four buttons. The top button had a keyhole in it; the others were:

# E
# S
# L

According to a lit panel above the door, they were currently on S<sup>LEEP</sup>USTENANCE, but they soon dropped smoothly down to L<sup>IBRARY</sup>ABRATORY. There was nothing rosy about L: it was as bright as an operating room, so bright Darryl had to squint as he followed Mr. Masterly into a sleek, eight-sided room. The entire ceiling glowed. Again there were no windows, but each of the eight sides had a door. In the center of the room was an octagonal console with eight computer stations, at one of which an Asian girl with long, lustrous black hair was eating a sandwich. Except for her, and the plaques on the doors and the Paradise Lab screen savers on the monitors, the only thing in the octagon that wasn't gleaming white was a globe of red glass mounted on a pole above the console.

"Darryl, meet Suki," Mr. Masterly said.

"Hi, Darryl," the Asian girl said, wiping her mouth with a napkin.

"Nice to meet you," Darryl said.

"Any nibbles, Suki?" Mr. Masterly asked.

"Not today, sir."

"Once you're accepted here, Darryl, you have the

run of the place, twenty-four hours a day. We have no locks in Paradise, do we, Suki?"

"Of course not, sir."

Darryl glanced curiously at the elevator, which had the keyhole in the top button, but Mr. Masterly pointed at the next door over, labeled Emergency. "Stairs, in case the elevator breaks down. Though that never happens."

Mr. Masterly showed him through the third door, marked Books, and it was like traveling back in time. A long mahogany library table with green-globed student lamps was flanked by bookshelves so tall that there were sliding mahogany ladders for reaching the top shelves. The only modern touch was the computers in the study carrels.

"How many books are in here, sir?" Darryl asked, wide-eyed.

"You tell me."

Darryl quickly counted the books on one shelf, the number of shelves in each case, and estimated the number of cases.

"Ten thousand?"

"Very close. It's our scientific library."

Darryl came up with a similar estimate of the number of tapes in the next chamber, which was called Video. The tapes were of lectures and demonstrations given by the greatest scientific minds of their time. The next room, Bio, was a laboratory where high-powered microscopes were arrayed on stainless-steel tables flanked by shelves holding everything from slide racks and tweezers to glass jars containing dead frogs and pig fetuses suspended in formaldehyde. At the far end of Bio were stacks of cages containing crusty old white rats and what looked like aquariums, except with insects flitting around inside instead of fish.

"Fruit flies?" Darryl guessed.

"Exactly," Mr. Masterly said.

Next came Chem, another laboratory, with Bunsen burners, and racks of test tubes, and nozzled tanks, and more microscopes, and a device for X-ray crystallography, and setups for chemical experiments with rubber and glass tubes connecting beakers with various colored liquids in them. Here the shelves held brown glass jars labeled with the names of chemical compounds, acids, and elements, along with tanks containing gasses. In the rear of the room was what looked like a big, sunken, stainless-steel bathtub, for mixing chemicals.

The next room, Accel, was dominated by what looked like a gigantic steel beehive.

"A circular accelerator, for splitting atoms," Mr. Masterly said.

When they came to the last door, marked Snoodles,

Mr. Masterly knocked. It was opened by a stooped old man with a crescent-shaped scar on his forehead.

"S-s-sorry, s-s-sirs!" he stammered, shuffling out in a droopy white lab coat. "I thought p-p-people was at lunch. Want me to cook up some more of that p-p-polliwog?"

"Polymer," Mr. Masterly gently corrected him. "No, I just wanted you to meet Darryl Kirby. He may be joining us. If you need toxic chemicals mixed, Darryl, or need your microscope cleaned, Snoodles is your man. He keeps things shipshape."

"S-s-snoodles, at your s-s-service," the elderly man said, bowing. "Twenty-s-s-seven hours a day."

"Twenty-four," Mr. Masterly murmured.

"S-s-sorry, s-s-sir," Snoodles said, bamming his forehead with the heel of his hand. "I'm s-s-such a knucklehead."

After saying good-bye to Suki and the stammering old man, Mr. Masterly led Darryl back into the elevator, and they quickly swooshed up to E. The most spectacular gym Darryl had ever seen, EXERCISE ENTERTAINMENT was windowless, too, but bathed in a soft yellow light, as if morning sun was slanting down from the high, scaffolded ceiling. Mr. Masterly introduced him to an extremely muscular man in a gym suit who was mopping the rubber mat in the free-weight area.

"Darryl, Abs. Abs, Darryl Kirby."

Abs quit mopping to shake Darryl's hand, nearly crushing it. His biceps were as big around as Darryl's waist.

"Abs will help you with your fitness program. Won't you, Abs?"

Grinning broadly, Abs nodded his head, which had the same sort of scar on the forehead as Snoodles's. After giving Darryl's arm a squeeze, Abs grinned even more broadly, as if to say that there was plenty of room for improvement there. Then he led them onto a gleaming hardwood basketball court, where he picked up a loose basketball and swished it from forty feet. In the gymnastics area Abs performed flawless routines on the rings and the parallel bars and the pommel horse, never breaking a sweat, and on the tennis court he jumped the net to shake hands with an invisible opponent. In the cardiovascular center he demonstrated the treadmills and stair climbers and rowing machines, and in the strength-training center he ran through the state-of-the-art muscle-building machines. He didn't jump into the sparkling Olympic-sized swimming pool or the whirlpool bath beside it, but in the track-and-field area he ran a sprint and heaved a discus and threw a javelin the entire length of the field.

Leaving the gym, the three of them passed under an

archway with the word AquaFilm pulsing over it in aquamarine neon. Looming before them was a white ball, over fifty feet in diameter. Above it, suspended from the ceiling, was a platform reached by a two-way escalator rising up like one of those conveyor belts for carrying grain up into grain silos.

"What is that thing?" Darryl asked, eyeing the huge ball.

"Come see," Mr. Masterly said.

Normally Darryl wouldn't have stepped onto the narrow escalator for the world, but now he calmly rode all the way up to the platform with Abs and Mr. Masterly. On the platform a dozen clear-plastic containers were grouped like the petals of a flower around a central hole. They looked like big eggs, or small blimps, each about six feet long and three feet high, each with a foot pedal in front, a seat and steering wheel in the middle, what looked like a scuba diver's tank in the rear, and rotors and rudders mounted on the tails. Mr. Masterly unplugged the front egg—they all seemed to be charging—and lifted the lid on its top.

"Hop in," he said.

"What are they, sir?" Darryl asked.

"I call them movie pods."

"Movie pods?"

They were a bit reminiscent of the Space Needle's

elevators, and normally Darryl wouldn't have gotten near one. But normally he would have been a wreck just being up on that dizzying platform.

Abs deposited Darryl into a pod as if he weighed nothing.

"The pedal controls rotor speed," Mr. Masterly said, fastening Darryl's seat belt. "The whole thing lasts about ninety minutes. When it's over, just steer back up to the top. If I'm not here, Abs will be. Have fun!"

Before Darryl could ask *what* lasted ninety minutes, Mr. Masterly closed and sealed the pod's lid. The pod slid forward and tilted down and plopped through the hole into the top of the huge sphere. Suddenly everything was darker than BJ's basement room at night—and for a second Darryl actually pictured BJ. But BJ seemed far, far away, the inhabitant of another world, and the thought of him slipped away like a space eel.

Though Darryl was all alone, locked in a clear egg that seemed to be slowly sinking in the darkness, he felt surprisingly calm. He experimented with the steering wheel and the pedal. By pressing the pedal, he increased the rotor speed, and the pod seemed to rise. Easing off the pedal decreased rotor speed, and the pod sank.

It dawned on him that the huge round ball was actually a tank of water, and for a moment, as glimmers of color began to dart by his see-through submarine, he thought they were tropical fish. But in fact they were just flickers of light. The flickers grew brighter; off to his right the water took on a brilliant green glow. Intrigued, Darryl turned the wheel that way and pressed the pedal halfway down. As he approached the glow, it came into focus, becoming a primeval forest full of trees even more exotic than the monkey puzzle in his old backyard. As he neared the treetops, two gigantic birds leaped off a branch and flew right at him, the flapping of their wings deafening in his ears. He jerked the wheel to the left and floored the pedal. The birds whizzed past the pod, barely missing it. Except they weren't birds at all. They were pterodactyls.

Darryl guided the pod back out into the middle of the tank. He quickly recovered from the shock of the attack of the winged dinosaurs and steered his little submarine toward a reddish-brown glow that resolved itself into a volcanic crater with a bubbly surface. When a jet of molten plasma spat right at him, Darryl jerked the wheel to the right and sped back to the middle of the tank. But before long a bluish glow lured him down and to the left. A lagoon. As he hovered above it, something gurgled; then a bizarre shape broke the surface: the head of a dinosaur with a breathing hole on a bump on its forehead. This time Darryl didn't flee.

The lagoon supported an astonishing variety of life

forms, ranging in size from dragonflies to bronto-
sauruses. In his clear pod Darryl felt as if he was part of
the ecosystem, and he got so caught up in every nook
and cranny of it that before he knew it, the hour and a
half was over and the tank turned dark again, leaving only a ring of red light at the top of the tank. He
guided his pod up toward it.

When the pod plopped back onto the platform,
there stood Mr. Masterly. He unsealed the lid and
opened it.

"But I only saw the lagoon!" Darryl cried. "Can I go
back and see something else?"

"You liked it?"

"It's fantastic! How in the world does it work?"

"Well, the tank's made of a special nondistorting
Plexiglas we developed at MasterTech. The exterior's
sprayed with a special material used for rear-projection
movie screens. We use six different projectors. Needless
to say, it's a wildly expensive format, but the great thing
is, you can see it over and over without getting bored.
Or you don't have to watch the movies at all. Some of
the kids like just to ride around and enjoy the light
show. We have some kinks to work out with the sound
system, but it's coming along."

"I don't know why I stuck to that lagoon. There was
so much to see! Can you run it again?"

"Once you're through orientation, you can come back any night after dinner."

"Really?"

"Absolutely."

"What's orientation?"

"It basically brings you up to speed on the work we're doing here. That is, if you're interested in joining us."

"The work about . . . communicating with the dead?"

"Among other things."

"Are there more openings? My friend BJ's top of his class."

"I'm afraid there's just one at the moment. And if you take it, I'm also afraid you'll have to cut off ties to those you knew. As I said, we're top secret."

Darryl thought of BJ and his mother. But they seemed as distant as the Vulpecula galaxy.

"I suppose you could have one more go," Mr. Masterly said. "Pop into this pod over here. It's charged up, with a full air supply."

Darryl hopped eagerly into another pod. "Thanks!" he said, scrunching down so Mr. Masterly could seal him in.

"**C**ops!" Ronnie Johnson cried.

As a squad car nosed into the parking lot, kids scattered in all directions. Big T sprinted up Cedar Street, but BJ headed in the exact opposite direction: due west, across the glinting railroad tracks. A siren wailed. But BJ had Big T's number-two board, and once he was sailing along in the shade of the Alaska Way Viaduct, the wailing at his back diminished. It seemed only fair that the police weren't chasing *him*. He'd felt a twinge of envy watching Big T pry the silver jaguar off the hood of that car, but he'd just stood around with his hands in his pockets, an innocent spectator.

At the aquarium BJ hopped off the board and hoofed it back across the tracks to the public elevator to the Pike Place Market. Up in the market the Korean guy at the fruit stand eyed him warily as he walked by, though *he* hadn't been the one to rip off a banana when the gang swaggered through the arcade an hour ago. He passed the fish throwers and the big piggy bank his mother dropped change into. When he got to First Avenue, he headed south, toward Pioneer Square, where you could get a bus up Yesler Way. He skulked along in the shadows of the buildings on the west side of the street, hoping to go unspotted by anyone who knew his mother.

It didn't surprise him to see somebody curled up asleep in the doorway of a boarded-up Army-Navy store. First Avenue was the original Skid Row, so named because in the old days they dragged skids of logs down to the waterfront on it, and bums and derelicts had always hung out there. But BJ was surprised that the sleeper looked familiar. He stepped into the doorway for a closer look. Stretched out on a sheet of cardboard was the scrawny boy with the ponytail and the tattoo who'd disappeared out the window at the Masterly Children's Shelter. BJ squatted down and gave him a shake. Boris shot up like a rocket. BJ lunged for his ankle. Boris was too quick.

But the sidewalk wasn't crowded, and thanks to his board, BJ was able to catch the weasel and pin him against the smoky-brick wall of an SRO hotel.

"What'd I freakin' do to you, man?" Boris muttered.

"You stole my friend's GameMaster. Remember?"

"That's years ago."

"It was a month ago."

"So what?"

This was a good question. What did BJ care about

Darryl and his GameMaster? In a month Darryl hadn't bothered to call once. He was surprised he'd even referred to him as a friend.

"Jeez, man, you need a bath," BJ said.

"Sorry. I ain't stayin' at the Ritz."

BJ relaxed his grip on Boris's arms. "Listen. If I let go, will you chill a minute?"

"Sure."

BJ let go of him—and Boris bolted. BJ snagged his sweatshirt. As Boris tried to slip out of it, BJ grabbed him around the neck.

"Let go or I'll yell for the cops!"

"Go ahead," BJ said.

But of course Boris didn't.

"Look, man, I just wanted to know if you found your sister yet."

"What's it to you?"

"Just curious."

"Nah. I was up in Bellingham last week, but it was a bust."

"You lost her down in Portland, right?"

"That's where we ran out of gas. We was thinking about Canada."

"Your sister can drive?"

"Nah, she's just twelve. I was driving."

"You can drive in Oregon when you're fourteen?"

"Nah, I kiped my dad's car so we could run away. Hot-wired it."

"Huh," BJ said, not sure he believed this. "So you ended up in a shelter and your sister just disappeared?"

"I figure somebody started beating on her like you're doing to me. So she split. What's it to you?"

"Just it's kind of strange. Darryl disappeared, too."

"The GameMaster guy?"

"Yeah."

"You're killin' my neck."

BJ let go of him.

"It is kind of weird, them two both disappearing," Boris said, this time staying put. "The two whizzes."

"Have you checked to see if your sister went home to your dad?"

Boris snorted. "No way she'd do that. But yeah, I checked one time. Had this girl I met call and ask for her. My old man hadn't seen her in months. Not that he cared."

Smelly as Boris was, BJ was beginning to feel for him. "How long you been sleeping on the streets?"

"Who knows?" Boris pulled a beetle out of his greasy hair and squashed it between his fingers. "Tell you the truth, I was thinking I might go back to that shelter for a few days. Rest up, get a shower."

"Let's go."

"Now?"

"We can catch a bus to Madrona down in Pioneer Square. I'll go with you."

Half an hour later BJ was ditching his board under the hedge of old rhododendrons bordering the shelter's gravel drive. The sneering redhead, still not placed, was sprawled on the porch glider when they walked up.

"P-U," she said.

"You don't smell like no rose petals yourself," Boris snapped.

"Where's Ms. Grimsley?" BJ asked.

"Probably in the garage sniffing the bucket seats in her new car," said the redhead.

But BJ found Ms. Grimsley reading in her office.

"Mr. Walker," she said, shoving her paperback into her bag. "Surely it's not Saturday."

"No. I brought Boris."

"Hey," Boris said, stepping in. "I was wondering if I could stay a few days."

"We're not a hotel, Mr. Rizniak."

"But he's been living on the streets," BJ said. "You're not full up, are you?"

"Not at the moment, no."

In the end she grudgingly agreed to let Boris have a room—the same third-floor room he'd shared with Darryl a month ago. BJ accompanied him up there.

"She didn't know about the knife?" Boris said, closing the door.

"Nah," said BJ.

"Thanks, man. Where is it?"

"I got it at home."

"Can I have it back?"

"When you cough up Darryl's GameMaster."

"I had to sell it for bus tickets."

BJ sat down at the desk. "Do me a favor, will you?"

"What?"

"Take a shower."

"You're the one stinking the place up."

But in a minute Boris actually did traipse out of the room.

Left on his own, BJ flicked on the laptop—the real reason he'd come. Ever since he'd watched Darryl play StarMaster, CastleMaster had seemed kind of lame, but on his Saturday visits here he never had time to try his luck, what with his mother waiting in the car. He'd forgotten about the maze, though. This one looked disturbingly complex. But he concentrated on visualizing a path through it, and with a couple of lucky guesses he managed to make it through with five seconds to spare.

The game list appeared, and he clicked on StarMaster 3. His opponent was called SuperSuk. He just called himself BJ. But he wasn't experienced and had recruited only two Individualist leaders when Boris came back in—smelly as ever.

"You didn't shower?"

"Keep your shorts on. I wanted to check out Grimface's new wheels. You're not gonna believe what she's driving."

"What?"

"A brand-new S-GPS 600."

"A Mercedes?"

"No, a toaster oven. What do you think, dork-brain?"

"But they're top of the line."

"No duh. Come on, man, you got to check it out."

So BJ gave up the losing cause and went to see Ms. Grimsley's fancy new car.

## 15

As soon as she opened her eyes, she shut them again and tried to get back to the circus tent. She'd just let go of her trapeze; she'd been somersaulting through the air to the astonished gasps of the crowd below. A tiny figure was swinging toward her, hanging by his knees from another trapeze, growing bigger and bigger the closer they got. It was Boris! She flew toward him, but when she grabbed his hands, she couldn't quite hold on, and the crowd sucked in its breath. Yet even as she tumbled through the air, she knew she would land in the safety net, and soon Boris would drop down and join her there and the relieved crowd would give them a hand anyway.

However, she landed in her bed. She wasn't a daredevil flying-trapeze artist at all, she was just Nina Rizniak, twelve and blind as a bat. And she wasn't with her brother, she was all alone in room seven at Paradise Lab. Most mornings she managed not to cry, but the feel of her brother's hands, brief as it had been, seemed so real that she couldn't keep her eyes from misting over, making the rosy blur of the globe light turn to tomato soup.

The soup brightened as Mr. Masterly's recorded voice filled the room:

"Rise and shine, friend and colleague. It's a new day—the day you may well make the discovery that will change human history. . . ."

Nina put a pillow over her head, muffling the inspirational voice. Long after the daily pep talk ended, she was still trying to get a grip on herself. But finally, knowing she would be the last to breakfast, she tossed the pillow aside and climbed down out of the luxurious bed and put on her glasses.

Eyeing her from across the plush room was a young acrobat. She'd happened across the painting, by Picasso, a couple of months ago, while surfing through Art on her remote, and she'd left it up ever since because it reminded her of Boris.

Picking up the remote, she went to Music, and soon her favorite song filled the room. She'd found it, too, by chance, while surfing through Campfire Songs.

*When the world is gloomy and glum,*
*I only know one thing to do;*
*I remember the moon and the sun*
*And then I remember you. . . .*

The moon and the sun, she thought as the wall panel slid back and she walked into the blue-tiled bathroom.

How wonderful it would be to see Boris and the out-doors again! Then they could join the circus and become the Flying Rizniaks, just as they'd planned. And he would get her contact lenses, as he'd promised, so she wouldn't have to worry about her glasses falling off when she was somersaulting through midair. They would become famous and make a fortune, but when their father came to beg money from them, Boris would pretend not to know him, and when their father said, "But I'm your father!" Boris would say, "The one who beat me with his belt?" If their father denied it, they would give him nothing, but if he admitted it, they would give him a thousand dollars, so long as he prom-ised never to come begging again. And she and Boris would buy a house so big, they could practice their tra-peze act in the living room, and there would be a whole wing for their hamsters and gerbils and monkeys and dogs and cats and parakeets and turtles. . . .

Her mood entirely changed, Nina bounced out of the dressing room in a sky-blue jumpsuit and sun-yellow jelly shoes, her face washed, teeth brushed, curly blond hair combed as well as it could be. But once she left room seven and the hopeful song behind, her mood soured.

She trudged down the carpeted corridor into the dining hall. When she'd first joined the others here after her orientation, the dining table had been oval shaped, but a couple of months ago a new one had replaced it, shaped irregularly, like a cross section of the G-17 molecule. As she took her place there—things at Paradise Lab tended to be numbered, and there was a 7 on the back of her chair—six of the seven kids already there regaled her with a chipper chorus of "Morning, Nina."

"Morning, everybody," she said, doing her best to sound chipper back.

The kitchen door swung open, and out shuffled Hedderly with a steaming platter of scrambled eggs. He gave it to Ruthie Katz, who was eighteen and sat at the head of the table.

"Very good, Hedderly," Ruthie said in the tone a parent would use on a small child.

Hedderly wasn't a small child. He was a balding, two-hundred-fifty-pound man. But as with Abs and Snoodles, there was something docile and childlike about him. He had the same vacant eyes and the same crescent-moon scar on his forehead.

After spooning herself a portion of scrambled eggs, Ruthie passed the platter to Mario Hernandez in chair number two. Though small for his age, Mario was seventeen. He took some eggs and passed them to sixteen-year-old Billy O'Connor, who had flaming red hair and flaming red pimples. In chair number four sat Paul

Pettinio, who was fifteen and, in spite of Abs's efforts to get him to do calisthenics, extremely fat. Chair number five was Suki Yamashita, also fifteen, with long, straight, jet-black hair that Nina envied. Next came Greg Birtwissel, the prissy fourteen-year-old in chair number six, who passed the eggs on to Nina. She spooned some onto her plate and passed them on to the boy with messy dirty-blond hair in chair number eight—the one who hadn't said "Morning, Nina," probably because he didn't know her name. She'd seen him a couple of times with Abs up on E, but he'd been in orientation, so she hadn't bothered trying to make conversation, even though he looked about her age. This was the first time he'd joined the rest of them for a meal—the first time since she'd come here that she hadn't been the last served.

Hedderly shuffled back out of the kitchen with a basket of muffins.

"Blueberry?" Ruthie said, taking the basket. "No bran?"

"Sorry, miss."

Ruthie clucked her tongue.

"I'll eat yours," Paul volunteered.

But Ruthie took a muffin and passed them on. When they reached Suki, Hedderly reappeared carrying a plate heaped with crisp strips of bacon. He could easily have brought the bacon and muffins in one trip, but things like that never seemed to occur to him.

At each of the eight places a tall glass of fresh-squeezed orange juice towered over a small, pale-blue vitamin tablet. Once they were all served and Hedderly shuffled away, Ruthie lifted her glass.

"To conquering Time!"

"Conquering Time!" the others chimed in—all except the new boy, who got it out a couple of seconds late, like an echo.

They swallowed their vitamins—all except Nina, who pretended to pop the vitamin into her mouth but in fact palmed it and slipped it into the pocket of her jumpsuit. Then they dug into their eggs—all except the new boy, who started with his bacon.

"Eggs first," Nina murmured.

"Excuse me?" the new boy said.

"Eggs first, because they get cold fastest," she said, repeating what Greg Birtwissel had told her on her first day at the team table. "Bacon second. Muffins last."

"Oh. Thanks."

He set down the strip of bacon and attacked the eggs. Once they were all on their muffins, the kitchen door swung open again. But this time it wasn't Hedderly.

"Good morning, Mr. Masterly!" they all cried—again with the new boy a beat behind the rest.

Mr. Masterly stood behind Ruthie's chair, his hands on her shoulders, and even in the rosy lighting you could tell she was blushing with pleasure.

"It is a good morning," he said. "We're now eight strong—a new record."

"A new record!" several of them murmured appreciatively.

"Stand up, will you, Darryl?"

The new boy jumped to his feet, his napkin drifting to the floor.

"You've probably seen him around, but for those of you who haven't met him yet, this is Darryl Kirby, your newest colleague."

"Hi, Darryl," came a chorus from around the table.

"Hi," Darryl said.

"Darryl, this is Ruthie Katz," Mr. Masterly said, and then he went around the table, naming everyone. "And last but not least," he concluded, "Nina Rizniak. Nina's only a few months older than you."

Darryl gave her such a strange look that Nina wiped her lips with her napkin, thinking maybe they had blueberry on them.

"Darryl's going to be an invaluable addition to the team," Mr. Masterly went on. "I have high hopes for a breakthrough on the G-17 project in the next few weeks. Tell them what you know about G-17, Darryl."

"G-17 is a complex polymer that modifies the human DNA chain so that certain cells don't degenerate and other cells that don't normally replicate will."

"And what is the problem we're having with it?"

"It's not a totally stable compound. Its structure is kind of fragile, so it breaks down when exposed to certain amino acids in the DNA. Then it stops working."

"Thank you, Darryl. I've got some business to attend to now, but I'll be joining you later down on L."

"See you, sir," came a chorus from the table as Mr. Masterly left by the door to the hall.

"Sounds like you enjoyed the mall," Nina murmured as Darryl sat back down.

"The mall?"

"Orientation. I call it that because, you know, it's all about molecules. Get it? Mall, molecules."

But Darryl didn't laugh, not seeming to get the joke.

## 16

As soon as BJ got home from the shelter, he grabbed the phone and phone book and led a parade of cats down to the basement. He looked up a number in the business pages and dialed it.

"Good afternoon, Bellevue Imports," a woman said.

"Could I have the sales department, please?" BJ said, trying to sound grown-up.

He must have succeeded, for the woman said, "Certainly, sir."

A syrupy-voiced man came on the line. "Good morning. Jerry McPherson here, what can I do for you?"

"I'm calling about the Mercedes we bought from you recently," BJ said, plunking down on the bottom bunk. "We've only put two hundred miles on it and there's already a rattle."

"A rattle? That's unusual—highly unusual. What's your name?"

"Grimsley."

"Grimsley, Grimsley . . . with a G?"

"Yes."

"I don't see any Grimsley. Are you sure you bought it here?"

It had definitely said Bellevue Imports on the license-plate frames of the sleek new Mercedes Boris had just shown him in the shelter's garage. Maybe it hadn't been bought in Ms. Grimsley's name.

"This is North Seattle Imports, isn't it?" BJ said.

"This is Bellevue Imports."

"Oh, gosh, I'm sorry."

After hanging up, he lay down on the bunk and thought so hard, he barely felt it when Booker T and Aristotle jumped up and started kneading his T-shirt. After about five minutes he jerked back into a sitting position and hit the redial button.

"Good afternoon, Bellevue Imports," said the same woman's voice.

"Hello, this is Sergeant Walker from the Seattle Police Department," BJ said, making his voice extra deep. "We stopped a speeder this morning and it turned out he had no registration for the car he was driving. We suspect it's stolen, but nobody's reported it missing yet. It's a brand-new Mercedes from Bellevue Imports. Forest-green sedan, tan upholstery, S-GPS 600. We were hoping to get the owner's name from you."

"Let me see, forest-green S-GPS 600. According to our records, the only forest-green sedan we've sold recently was . . . good grief, I wonder if this can be right."

"You have the buyer's name?"

"Well, it *says* Keith Masterly. Do you suppose it's *the* Keith Masterly? But didn't he report the missing car to you? It *is* an S-GPS Special."

BJ grunted as if he knew what this meant, thanked her, and hung up, wondering why in the world Keith Masterly would buy Ms. Grimsley a car. She worked at a Masterly Children's Shelter, true—but a new Mercedes 600?

*The two whizzes.* GameMasters, MondoGameMasters, Masterly Children's Shelters. And now Keith Masterly himself!

BJ popped up, sending Booker T sprawling. Among the articles pasted up over his table was one including a picture of Keith Masterly with his son, Keith Jr. According to the caption, Keith Jr. was sixteen, but the article was two years old. He would now be eighteen— on the verge of leaving home, most likely. Could it be that Keith Masterly liked having a son around and had adopted Darryl? Maybe he'd heard how good Darryl was at GameMaster through the person in Darryl's family who'd worked for MasterTech. If Darryl was living in that fabulous place across the lake, who could blame him for not calling!

"I've got to find out, Confucius," BJ said to the runty cat rubbing the side of his head against his ankle.

## 17

After breakfast Darryl followed the rest of the team down to L, his first visit there since Mr. Masterly's guided tour. During his month of orientation he'd made a daily trip to E to get some exercise with Abs, but the rest of his time had been spent in room eight with Mr. Masterly—or, more accurately, with Mr. Masterly's voice and image.

Every morning had begun the same way, the rosy glow brightening as Mr. Masterly's voice filled the room:

"Rise and shine, friend and colleague. It's a new day—the day you may well make the discovery that will change human history. Of course brilliant minds have been trying to outfox Time for years. So why should I think you can succeed where older and more experienced minds have failed? For that very reason: You're *not* old and experienced. Your mind is still young and supple, unset in its ways. Experience can be a hindrance as well as a help. It can narrow your scope, blind you to possibilities. I believe it will be a truly open mind, a young and fertile and vigorous mind, that will make the great connection, take the great leap. Imagine, living without the sword of Time hanging over your head! And imagine being more famous, more acclaimed, more celebrated than Thomas Edison and Isaac Newton and Christopher Columbus rolled into one! That will be your fate if you solve the mystery. And I truly believe *you* can be the one to do it."

By the time Darryl washed his face and brushed his teeth and decided which color jumpsuit he felt like wearing, Hedderly would have rolled in breakfast on a cart. It was always scrumptious. Once Darryl cleaned his plate, Mr. Masterly's face would appear on the wide screen.

"Sleep well?" he would say with a smile.

"Like a rock," Darryl would reply, not thinking it the least bit silly to talk to a screen.

"Enjoy your breakfast?"

"It was great!"

"Take your vitamin?"

"Yes!"

Then Mr. Masterly would say, "Ready to dip into the periodic table?" or "Ready to learn more biochemistry?" or "Ready to move on to theories of gene therapy?" Whereupon Darryl would say, "Sure!" and sit there like a human sponge, absorbing every word, every concept, every equation.

The final few sessions had been about G-17, and now that he was down on L with the others, he was eager to see the interesting molecule for himself. He asked Ruthie if he could look at it under a microscope.

"*Snoodles!*" she cried.

Ruthie had a shrill, penetrating voice, and Snoodles quickly came shuffling out of his quarters.

"S-s-sorry!" he cried. "S-s-snoozing again!"

"Prepare a slide of G-17 and set up the electron microscope for Darryl."

"Right away, miss!"

Darryl followed the stooped, stuttering man into the rear of Chem and watched him attach a hose to the nozzle of a gray tank and start filling the mixing tank. When the big sunken bathtub was about a third full of a grayish liquid, Snoodles turned the valve and hooked the hose up to an orange tank and started adding an orange liquid to the gray. Soon the vat was two thirds full of a liquid the color of root beer. Then he unscrewed the lids of three brown-glass jars and, using a long-handled measuring spoon, dumped eight cups of a white powder and six cups of canary-yellow granules into the vat. With tongs he pulled a crystal out of the third jar and tossed it in with the rest. Next, he switched the hose to another tank and injected some gaseous bubbles; then he flipped a wall switch and a gigantic version of the mixing blade on Darryl's grand-mother's mixer descended from the ceiling and whipped the contents of the vat into a froth. When the mixing was done and the froth settled, the liquid in the tank was as green as a frog's back—except for one tiny blue freckle that kept popping around the surface like a drop of grease in a scalding saucepan. Snoodles leaned over the tub with an eyedropper, and when the tiny blue freckle scooted over near him, he sucked it up. He then flipped a switch on the side of the vat, and the vat turned into an oversized version of an airplane toilet, the bottom dropping out like a trapdoor and cleanser swirling around the sides, flushing out all the green liquid. Once the vat was empty, the bottom flipped back into place.

Snoodles shuffled over to the counter and squeezed the tiny blue freckle of liquid out of the eyedropper onto a slide, over which he placed an ultra-thin strip of glass. Carrying the slide before him like a candle, he shuffled from Chem to Bio and slipped it in place in an electron microscope.

"There you go, young s-s-sir."

In spite of all the work that had gone into producing the slide, Darryl climbed onto the tall stool and peered into the microscope without bothering to thank the elderly man. At first all he could see were his own eyelashes magnified. But when he adjusted the focus knob, he caught his breath. There it was, in all its glory—G-17! He'd memorized its molecular structure in orientation, but this was the thing itself, the actual constellation of atoms.

He could have marveled at its complexities all day, but after a while he heard Mr. Masterly's voice and jumped off his stool and dashed out into the octagon. It was deserted: everyone was crowded into Chem.

"Ah, Darryl, thank you for joining us," said Mr. Masterly, who was standing at a stainless-steel counter, his right hand resting on a small chest. It hadn't been there when Snoodles was preparing the slide. "I was just saying how even though I'm well past my mental prime—"

"No, you're not!" a chorus of young voices protested.

Mr. Masterly smiled. "It's sad but true. Nevertheless, I did have an idea of sorts the other day. We're looking to find a durable structure for G-17, one that doesn't disintegrate over time. So why shouldn't we study the most durable thing to occur naturally on earth?"

"Iron?" Ruthie piped up.

"Even more durable than iron."

"Titanium?" said Suki.

"Good guess. But . . . "

Mr. Masterly opened the lid of the chest, and everyone gasped.

"Diamonds!" they said in hushed unison.

Mr. Masterly dug out a handful of the glittering gems and let them sift back into the chest as if they were grains of wheat. "Highest quality. Feel free to play around with them. Who knows, something in their molecular structure may give us a hint." With that Mr. Masterly went out into the octagon, and they all followed as if he was the Pied Piper. "Sadly, I have to head back to town. But before I go, I want to congratulate Mario for coming up with an original and ingenious approach to G-17. Mario had the idea of freezing the molecule at minus one hundred degrees Celsius before injecting it into the DNA. Unfortunately, once the G-17 thawed out, it broke down again. But it worked for a little while—and it's the kind of innovative thinking I like. Before I came down here, I put a Mario trophy in the case."

Everybody applauded and clapped Mario on the back.

"Ah," Mr. Masterly said. "I see we have a player."

The red globe mounted on the pole atop the computer console had started flashing like the cherry on a police car.

"I'll take it," said Greg Birtwissel, manning one of the computers.

The flashing red light gave Darryl a weird, hollow

feeling in his gut—but only for a moment. "What's it mean?" he asked.

"Someone made it through the maze," Mr. Masterly said.

The maze, Darryl thought, hazily remembering the MondoGameMaster in the shelter.

"What's their poison, Greg?" Mr. Masterly asked.

"MasterTrek," Greg said.

They all gathered around and watched as Greg typed in "Want to play?" A *Yes* soon appeared on the screen. Greg identified himself as FastFingers. The player identified herself as Rosalie_W. But Rosalie_W was no match for FastFingers. Greg was soon levels ahead.

"Pity," Mr. Masterly said. "But of course people as bright as you come along only once in a blue moon."

"Can anyone play?" Darryl asked.

"Sure."

"What happens if they beat us?"

"Ask Nina."

"You beat me at StarMaster," Nina said. "Two out of three."

"That was you?" Darryl said. "What did you call yourself?"

"NABATW," Nina said.

"What is that?"

"My handle. And you're MDK, right?"

Darryl nodded.

"If somebody gives you a real run for your money, hit control D," Mr. Masterly said. "Simple as that."

"I've been here for ages and I've never got to do it," Ruthie said with a sniff. "They're always so dumb and slow."

"Most are, sadly, but now and then we get an exception," Mr. Masterly said, bringing a glow to Darryl's face by patting him on the shoulder. "I'm afraid I'm off—much as I'd prefer to stay here and work on G-17 with you. Tell me. What's the worst thing we can do?"

"Waste time!" everyone said.

"Exactly."

As soon as Mr. Masterly left, Darryl dashed back into Bio to continue his scrutiny of G-17. He'd learned in orientation that the mysteries of life are locked up in DNA, the genetic building block, and that DNA is made up of various combinations of twenty-one different amino acids. For a year or two the work at Paradise Lab had been devoted to attempts to modify these amino acids, but their molecules had proven too complex to work with. G-17 wasn't quite so complex, but it was complex enough.

At twelve-thirty Ruthie led them back up to S for lunch—all but Paul Pettinio, who remained behind on game duty. After lunch the team returned to L and worked four more hours; then they trooped up to E. Till today Darryl had usually gone there when the others were on L, and he'd always done calisthenics with Abs. It hadn't occurred to him to do anything else. It hadn't occurred to him that he had a choice. But along with the gym suit and cross-training shoes in his personalized locker in the boys' locker room there was a swim suit, and seeing Mario change into one, he decided to do the same.

When he dove into the pool, a memory of the last time he'd swum—with BJ at Madison Beach—shot through his mind, but it was gone by the time he popped up for air. He and Mario swam laps for about twenty minutes; then they rested in the whirlpool bath. From there he could see Ruthie Katz wiping out Billy O'Connor in a game of one-on-one on the basketball court. Abs was showing Greg Birtwissel how to do curls in the free-weight area, Abs using eighty-pound barbells while Greg tried to imitate him with five-pounders. Paul Pettinio was on one of the Exercycles, but it must have been on the easiest setting, for his cottage-cheesy legs were moving in slow motion. Once Greg got the hang of curls, Abs went over to the track to help Suki with her javelin throwing. But it was Nina Rizniak, swinging on the rings in the gymnastics area, who snagged Darryl's attention. It really was a pretty impressive display—at least until her glasses fell off. After dropping down to find them, she headed for the girls' locker room. Soon Billy O'Connor kicked the basketball into the pool, and Ruthie shrugged and went off to the locker room as well. Before heading for the locker room himself, Darryl dried off and hopped over to the gymnastics area. He needed a stepladder to reach the rings, but after swinging for a minute he decided that tomorrow he would devote the gym period to them.

Once everyone was showered and dressed, they headed up to the dining hall, where Hedderly served them a delicious meal of salmon steaks and curlicue pasta mixed with broccoli spears. After that, most of them went up to E, to the AquaFilm. But much as Darryl liked the idea of floating around the prehistoric world in one of the movie pods, he was so exhausted that he could barely drag himself back to room eight.

## 18

Not once during the blurry month of orientation had Darryl been tempted to fool around with his remote control, but that night the sight of it gave him a second wind. He changed into pajamas, brushed his teeth, snuggled into the wonderful bed, and after scrolling through the movie choices picked one he'd never heard of called *Meteor Fiends*. He got about halfway through it before conking out.

"Rise and shine, friend and colleague. . . ."

Darryl's very first waking thought was of G-17. Maybe this would be the day he would stabilize it and become more famous than Isaac Newton and Albert Einstein and Christopher Columbus rolled into one! He jumped out of bed and washed his face and picked out a red jumpsuit, the color Mario had worn yesterday when everyone applauded him. On his way to breakfast he paused to check out the trophy case.

"Morning, Darryl."

Nina Rizniak stepped out from the shadows beyond the case, her jumpsuit the same robin's-egg blue as her slightly magnified eyes.

"See Mario's new trophy?" he said, pointing at a Mario-shaped figurine.

"I wanted to ask you something," she said, not even glancing at the case. "Yesterday morning you gave me a weird look when you heard my name. How come?"

"I'm not really sure. It seemed familiar, somehow. Your face, too."

"Where are you from?"

"Seattle. You?"

"Oregon. Down near Eugene."

"It's like . . . it's as if I know you from somewhere. But I can't remember where. My memory's a little . . ."

His whole past life seemed fuzzy and faraway. Looking back on it was like looking through the wrong end of a telescope. In fact, the people and events of his past seemed less real than the characters in *Meteor Fiends*. But he did his best to concentrate on Nina. She said he'd beaten her two out of three times at StarMaster. He'd played that on the laptop at the shelter. . . .

"Do you have a brother named Boris?"

Nina's face turned white as chalk. "You know Boris?"

"He stole my GameMaster."

"Where?"

"A children's shelter in Seattle."

"When?"

"Let me think. Gosh, it's hard to say. In July? What is it now?"

"The middle of August."

Oddly enough, he hadn't given a thought to what time of year it was—maybe because Paradise Lab had no windows. Would he have to go back to school in September?

"Boy, you really lose track of time in here, even though we're trying to conquer it."

"How was he?" Nina asked, her face still bloodless.

"Boris? I don't know. He took off out the window like a bird."

A smile bloomed on Nina's face, turning her quite pretty. "What do you expect, he's a Flying Rizniak. What did he say?"

"I think he showed me your picture."

"He did!"

"I think . . . he's looking for you. All over. Funny. And here you are."

A couple of magnified tears slipped out of her magnified eyes. She took off her glasses and wiped her face with a sleeve. "What else did he say?" she asked.

"I think he said you were good at GameMaster."

"Yeah, my friend Sue Ann had one."

Mario and Ruthie came out of doors farther down

the corridor and headed for the dining hall. "We better get to breakfast," he said.

"Will you do me one favor?" Nina whispered, grabbing his sleeve.

"What?"

"Don't take your vitamin."

"Why not? They're MasterPills."

"Don't take it. Just today. Okay? Pretend to, but slip it in your pocket."

"But that's the first thing you learn in orientation. A vitamin every morning gives you the added edge that might just make the difference."

"I know, I know. But . . . if you don't take it, I'll be your friend."

With that Nina headed for the dining hall. Darryl followed and took chair number eight, and soon Hedderly brought out a platter of sunny-side-up eggs. Then came a dish of link sausages, and finally a basket of cranberry muffins.

"To conquering Time!" Ruthie said, lifting her glass of fresh-squeezed grapefruit juice.

"Conquering Time!" the rest of them echoed.

They all reached for their pale-blue vitamins and popped them into their mouths and washed them down—all except Nina, who palmed her pill, and Darryl, who accidently dropped his. Nina ducked under the table and snatched it up. She lost her glasses in the process. Darryl grabbed those.

"Trade you," he whispered.

She shook her head. He turned to complain to Ruthie, but just at that moment Ruthie swiveled in her chair and cried shrilly:

"Hedderly! Some jam!"

Darryl swallowed his complaint and set Nina's glasses by her place mat, figuring it wouldn't kill him to miss his vitamin once.

**19**

<A>fter his mother left for work that morning, BJ rode up Twenty-third Street to Roanoke, where he locked his bike to the trunk of a skinny dogwood tree and joined a pair of nuns at the bus stop. The nuns wanted to know all about his school. He described Garfield but didn't mention that he was first in his class, as he would have before Darryl had taken him down a few pegs.

When the Bellevue bus pulled up and the friendly nuns didn't get on along with him, it seemed a bad sign. But he stuck to his plan. As soon as the bus had crossed the Evergreen Point floating bridge to the east side of the lake, he pushed the yellow strip, and the driver took the Hunt's Point exit. BJ got off and walked north, up Hunt's Point Road.

Most of the houses he passed were as big as the shelter, and by the time a high stucco wall loomed up on his right, he was wondering if maybe he should have worn something better than baggy jeans and a T-shirt. He stopped at a driveway blocked by what looked like a toll gate. A mustachioed man in a dark-red uniform emerged from a small guardhouse.

"Is this Keith Masterly's house?" BJ asked.

"Do you have an appointment?" the guard said doubtfully.

"No, I was—"

"The Masterlys don't like gawkers."

With that, the guard went back into the guardhouse and shut the door. BJ stepped up and knocked on the door.

"Yes?" the man said, opening the door partway.

"I just wanted to know if Darryl Kirby's here, sir," BJ said.

The guard stroked his impressive mustache as he consulted a clipboard. "No Kirbys with appointments today."

"I don't mean with an appointment. I mean living here."

"I only deal with appointments. Now don't make me have to ask you to leave again."

The guard shut the door in his face, leaving BJ no choice but to turn and slouch back up the road. Once he was out of sight of the guardhouse, he shinnied up a cedar growing by the stucco wall. But the top of the wall was encrusted with glinting shards of broken glass.

On the trudge back up Hunt's Point Road he figured he must have been right about the bad sign. Having to wait almost an hour for a bus back to Seattle didn't change his mind about this, nor did finding the seat of his bicycle covered with bird droppings. He rode home without sitting down, cleaned the seat, wolfed down a couple of ham sandwiches, then hopped back on his bike and rode to the shelter.

Ms. Grimsley was just coming out of her office as he walked into the front hall.

"Back again, Mr. Walker?"

"I just wanted to say hi to Boris, ma'am."

"Well, he was down for lunch, but I haven't seen him since."

"Could I check his room?"

"I suppose."

He climbed the two flights and found Boris asleep on the bed nearer the window.

"Catching up on your Z's?"

Boris leaped up, hands in karate position. BJ laughed and plunked down on the other bed.

"Where'd you get the new threads?"

Instead of filthy jeans and a sleeveless sweatshirt Boris had on a pair of khakis and a clean gingham shirt.

"Found 'em in a suitcase under the bed," Boris said. "What's happening?"

"I just wasted the whole day."

As BJ described his fool's errand across the lake, Boris opened the window, sat on the sill, pulled a pack of cigarettes from his sock, and lit up.

"Why'd you go over to Keith Masterly's house?" he asked, blowing smoke into the madrona.

"Guess who gave Grimface her fancy new car."

"Masterly?"

"Bingo."

BJ explained his theory of Darryl's adoption.

"Call up and ask, why don't you?" Boris said.

"Famous people like Masterly don't have listed numbers. But I've been thinking about what you said about your sister being a whiz at GameMaster, too. Maybe he adopted them both or something. I mean, you guys were at a Masterly shelter, too, right?"

"But how could he know they're so smart?"

BJ pointed at the laptop. "Did they have those in Portland?"

"Uh-huh."

"Maybe he's got them wired up to his house or something."

Boris took a thoughtful drag. "Maybe you're not as dumb as you look," he said, blowing smoke sideways out of his mouth. "How could we find out?"

"I was thinking about that on the bus back across the floating bridge. The property's on the lake. Maybe we could get at it from the water."

"You got a boat?"

"Yeah, we got a hundred-foot yacht with six masts."

"Okay, okay. You a good swimmer?"

"Not that good. Lake Washington's miles across. But . . . you know where the Seattle Yacht Club is? Just below the University? You can see it from the bridge."

"Where all them boats is parked?"

"Yeah. I figure we could borrow one."

"We?"

"Oh. So it was a lie, what you said about hot-wiring your dad's car?"

"That was no lie! I can hot-wire anything."

"Can you bust out of this place and be at the Yacht Club at noon tomorrow?"

"I can bust out of anywhere," Boris said, flicking his cigarette butt into the tree.

## 20

After lunch on his second day with the team, Darryl decided it would be a good idea to see how G-17 interacted with DNA, so he asked Snoodles to prepare him a slide containing both. Today, though, he felt a little embarrassed at having a stooped old man do things for him, so he followed Snoodles into Chem and watched closely so next time he could prepare the slide himself. And back in Bio, when Snoodles slipped the new slide into place in the microscope, Darryl said:

"Thanks a lot, Snoodles."

"Why, you're m-m-most welcome, young s-s-sir," Snoodles said, blinking in surprise.

Mr. Masterly wasn't around that day, so there were no interruptions, and Darryl spent the whole afternoon session studying the interaction of G-17 and DNA. The DNA seemed to glow at first, as if invigorated, but eventually the outer branches of the G-17 broke off, and the glow died.

Later, up on E, Darryl put on a gym suit instead of a swim suit and went to the gymnastics area. Abs showed him how to rosin his hands, then lifted him to the rings.

But as soon as Darryl started swinging, he was seized with panic.

Nina, who was on the pommel horse, saw him land on his butt. "You okay?" she asked.

"Yeah," he said, blushing. "I decided I felt more like swimming."

He ducked into the locker room, changed into his trunks, and spent the rest of the exercise period swimming laps.

After another delicious dinner—filet mignon and scalloped potatoes and string beans mixed with little pearl onions—he again skipped the movie in favor of bed. But like the night before, the sight of the remote perked him up. Instead of fast-forwarding to where he'd left off *Meteor Fiends*, he decided to catch a bit of the beginning to remind himself of the story, and it soon dawned on him that he hardly remembered it at all. He hadn't even realized it was a spoof! He must have been truly zonked last night to have taken it seriously. The meteor fiends were funny, not scary, and the way they talked—sort of like chipmunks—got him giggling.

But he soon stopped. Sitting there surrounded by his six satiny pillows, with twelve hundred movies and ten times that many songs at his fingertips, he began to feel lonely. Maybe it was because the movie *was* a comedy: laughing wasn't so much fun by yourself. Still, it was odd, for he hadn't felt lonely once since arriving here at Paradise, even though he'd spent more time by himself than ever before in his life.

He switched from *Meteor Fiends* to *Star Voyager*. But instead of getting swept up in the action, he thought of how it was BJ's favorite movie, too. BJ and Mrs. Walker . . . why hadn't he thought of them before? Or had he? Yes, he'd thought of them—but only as dim figures, like people he'd gone to kindergarten with or something. But now he could see BJ perfectly, in his droopy jeans and oversized T-shirt, and Mrs. Walker, with all her chins and jiggly arms and warm smile. She'd been so generous, feeding him and calling him "honey" and letting him sleep over. It had been a month since he'd seen them. Did they suppose he was dead? That he'd found a family he liked better and forgotten them?

He flicked off *Star Voyager* and stared disconsolately at the blank screen. He supposed he *had* found a new family of sorts, and *had* forgotten them. He'd never even thought of calling them. According to Mr. Masterly, Paradise Lab was in Washington State, so the call might not even be long distance, but it had never occurred to him to pick up a phone. He didn't know their number, but they were bound to be listed.

Come to think of it, he hadn't noticed any phones around Paradise. His room was fitted out with many luxuries, but he was pretty sure there was no telephone. He slipped out of bed and conducted a thorough search, even going through the drawers in the dressing room. No phone. No phone jack, either.

He changed out of his pajamas and put on a black jumpsuit and black jelly shoes and slipped out into the corridor.

"Night, Darryl," said Suki, who was just heading into room five.

"Have you seen a phone, Suki?" he asked.

"Nope. Sleep well."

She went into her room. Darryl walked down the corridor and checked the dining hall. Hedderly had cleared the dinner dishes and sponged off the table. No sign of a phone in there.

When he stepped into the elevator, Darryl felt queasy, and as soon as the door opened to E, he hustled out. Abs was in the weightlifting area, polishing the silver weights on the bench-press machine.

"Do you know where I could find a phone, Abs?"

Abs just grinned at him, shaking his head. Darryl walked past the pool and the deserted basketball court and the track and passed under the AquaFilm archway. The house lights were down, and the skin of the tank flickered with images of a prehistoric world. No sign of a phone.

He took the emergency stairs down to L and searched every nook and cranny except Snoodles's room. There were powerful computers, and state-of-the-art microscopes, and accelerators for subatomic particles, and X-ray defractors, and a chest full of diamonds—but no telephone. He flicked on one of the computers, thinking he might be able to email Mrs. Walker at the library. There was no Internet access.

As he peered around the deserted octagon, his breathing turned shallow. How could he have been so ungrateful after all BJ had done for him? Starting out with saving him from the switchblade of that crazy kid in the shelter. . . .

Boris Rizniak. By an amazing coincidence, Boris's sister was here in Paradise. She'd said if he didn't take the vitamin, she would be his friend. He'd had every intention of taking it: dropping it had been an accident.

Instead of waking poor Snoodles, Darryl took the stairs back up to S and went down the rosily lit corridor. He got no answer when he knocked on the door to room seven. Was Nina already asleep? Or up watching the AquaFilm?

"Night, Darryl."

Billy O'Connor, down the corridor, was about to go into room three.

"Is the movie over, Billy?"

"Just ended. Time for bed. Tomorrow may be the great day!"

Billy disappeared into his room. Darryl tried Nina's door. It opened. There were no locks in Paradise.

Her room looked identical to his. It appeared to be deserted.

"Nina?"

He rounded the foot of the bed. As he approached the far wall, a panel slid open, revealing a dressing room just like his.

"Nina?"

Where could she be? He went back down the corridor and, taking a deep breath, stepped into the elevator. His heart quickened as he pressed the top button, the one with the keyhole in it. Nothing happened.

Evidently there was one lock in Paradise.

He got out of the elevator and wandered back into the dining hall. Might there be a phone in the kitchen for Hedderly and the other staff members to call their families? He pushed open the swing door.

"Hi, Hedderly."

"Hi, boyo," said Hedderly, who was peeling potatoes.

"Is there a phone around?"

"A phone?"

"You know, a telephone."

"Not as I know of."

"A cell phone, maybe?"

"Not as I know of."

"Don't you ever call anybody?"

"Not as I know of."

Darryl walked into the dim pantry. To his right were towering shelves of canned goods; to his left, two steel doors: one big, one small. He opened the big one—and a blast of icy air swept over him. It was a vast freezer, with sides of beef and unscaled king salmon hanging from hooks and, in the back, great vats of ice cream. He closed that door and opened the little one. Inside was a boxlike chamber, room temperature, empty.

"What do you suppose it is?" he mumbled.

"I think it's a dumbwaiter."

Darryl whirled around. For a moment all he could see in the far corner of the pantry were two glimmering circles, but as he peered, the circles turned into the lenses on a pair of glasses.

"That's funny—I was hunting for you," he said. "What are you doing here?"

"Waiting," Nina said.

"For me?"

"Not exactly."

He looked into the small chamber, then back at her.

"Where's the waiter?"

"A dumbwaiter's a thing, not a person. It carries

food and stuff from one floor to another. It was in one of my mom's mysteries I read. They call it dumb because it doesn't talk, not because it's stupid."

"Where's this one go?"

"I don't know."

"So . . . what are you waiting here for?"

"Probably nothing. I waited twice before, but both times it was a bust."

He walked over to the dark corner. Next to where she was sitting there was a vent in the wall.

"What's that go to?"

"Have a look," she said, pulling off the vent cover. "I may be wrong, but I think there's only a minute to go."

She scrunched down and pushed herself into the horizontal vent on her back, headfirst.

"There's room for two," she said in an echoey voice.

He scrunched down, too, and pushed himself in beside her. It was a duct that bent upward after a few feet. As his shoulders reached hers, he sneezed.

"Dusty."

"Look up," she said.

He blinked and looked up. A long tube, less than a yard in diameter, stretched up and up and up—a hundred feet, it must have been—ending in a small black circle. He knocked on the tube. It was made of Teflon or some other hard plastic.

"What is it?"

"I think it's a ventilation pipe for the kitchen," she said. "See up there a few feet? That might be where the stove hooks in."

"But where does it go to?"

"Straight up. That's the sky."

"The sky? But it's getting . . ."

Nina sucked in her breath as the end of tube suddenly brightened.

"What's happening?" Darryl said.

"The moon!"

It didn't remain in place over the end of the tube very long. Maybe a minute. But it was definitely the moon—a full one.

After it slid away, they wormed their way out of the duct, and Darryl turned away from her. She'd seen him fall on his butt that afternoon: he didn't want her to see him crying now. For some reason, the sight of the moon had filled his eyes with tears.

He faked another sneeze, using it as an excuse to wipe his face. Then he saw that she had her glasses off and was wiping tears out of *her* eyes.

"How'd you know it would be there right then?"

"I made some calculations on one of the computers," she said. "And I hoped."

"Wow."

"I wonder if Boris was looking at it at the same time. . . ."

She'd put her glasses back on, but dim as it was, Darryl could see that her eyes were welling up again. He suddenly felt so sorry for her, being separated from her brother, that he put an arm around her. She leaned her head on his shoulder.

"I feel strange tonight," he said. "Different."

"Different from before you went to the mall?"

He giggled. The mall was such a silly name for orientation.

"I was hoping to see you tonight," she said. "I almost skipped the moon. I thought you might come by my room."

"I did."

"Really?"

"Do you know where there's a phone?"

She smiled sadly. "A phone."

"Yeah, it's so weird. I don't know why, but I never thought of calling my friends till now."

Nina said nothing. She just took his hand and gave it a squeeze.

## 21

The noon sun was blazing when BJ locked his bike to a lamppost outside the entrance to the Seattle Yacht Club. He waited in the shade of a cherry tree. After half an hour he was starting to mutter about how the weasel was no more dependable than Darryl when a clanking sound made him whip around. There Boris stood, a green toolbox at his feet.

"Where'd that come from?"

"I grabbed it. These nimrods at the Chevron station chased me about a mile out of my way. That's how come I'm late."

Squatting, BJ opened the toolbox. "This is great. It's got everything."

"Take me to the boats, man."

Boris looked surprisingly undisreputable in his borrowed clothes, but BJ, in cutoffs, figured it would be unwise to walk down the Yacht Club's driveway, what with a uniformed doorman standing under the clubhouse awning. So they skulked around the side of the Yacht Club grounds on the narrow lane leading down to Portage Bay. On the right was a funky shop plastered with signs advertising prices for renting boats and kayaks; on the left, the Yacht Club wall. The wall came to an end well above the water, so to reach the closest docks, all you had to do was scramble over some prickers. It was a weekday, and in spite of the balmy weather not many boats were out on the water, leaving the Yacht Club packed with sloops and yawls and ketches, cigarette boats and catamarans and cabin cruisers, Boston Whalers and three-masted schooners and a few yachts so big they had lifeboats on their decks like ocean liners.

"How about that guy?" Boris said, pointing at a cabin cruiser about fifty feet long. "The *Lazy Boy*."

"Too big," BJ said. "We don't want them to call out the Coast Guard or something."

"That one?" BJ pointed at a sleek little inboard-outboard with a fiberglass hull.

"Too flashy."

Boris plunked down on his toolbox, pulled a pack of cigarettes out of his sock, and lit up.

"What are you doing?" BJ said.

"What's it look like? I'm having a smoke while you figure out which boat we want."

But now that they were here, BJ couldn't go through with it. An image of his mother had loomed up like Quadros in CastleMaster.

"Maybe we should rent," he said.

"*Huh?*"

BJ dug nine dollars out of his pocket. "How much you got?"

"I'm busted."

"Yeah, right. How much did they give you for Darryl's GameMaster?"

"None of your friggin' business. But I just about got killed getting this." He patted the toolbox.

"Hide it," BJ said, turning away.

A bell tinkled as he went in the door to the rental shop. After the bright sunlight BJ couldn't see much in the shadowy place, but he could smell incense and varnish and soon made out an aging hippie with beads and long white hair who was varnishing one of those skinny boats they use in crew races.

"Peace, brother," the man said. "What can I do for you?"

"I want to rent a boat."

"How much you want to spend, brother?"

"I've got nine dollars."

The bell tinkled again as Boris sidled into the shop. "Peace, brother."

Boris looked at the man as if he was nuts.

"One-man kayak's eight bucks for the day," the man said.

"Can two people fit in it?" Boris asked.

"Sorry, brother. Two-man kayak's thirteen."

Boris reached into his left sock and produced a crumpled five-dollar bill. "I forgot about this," he said.

BJ took it and smoothed it out on the counter and handed over all but one dollar.

"Life vests are a buck each, brother."

"We got our own," said BJ.

"Kayak has to be back by six. And you have to leave a credit card."

"We don't have any credit cards."

"No credit card, no boat."

In spite of his brotherliness the old hippie was a cut-throat negotiator. Finally BJ had to get his bike and leave that and his watch, too.

The kayaks were in an open pen behind the shop: long, slender boats with scuffed fiberglass hulls and cockpits for the paddlers. BJ picked the newest-looking two-man.

"No way," Boris said. "I ain't going in no yellow boat."

"Okay, you pick."

Boris chose a red one with a black stripe. The paddles were all orange, so there could be no argument there. BJ grabbed two and lifted the front of the kayak while Boris picked up the rear. The proprietor opened a gate for them.

"You've kayaked before, right?" he said as they lugged the boat past him.

"Lots of times," BJ said.

Once the gate closed behind them, the two boys carried the kayak down to the water and set it in parallel to the shore. They ditched their shoes and socks under the brambles where Boris had hidden the toolbox.

"Gross," Boris said, stepping onto the slimy lake bottom.

"Get in front," BJ said.

"In your dreams."

"Fine, take the back."

But Boris soon popped out of the rear seat. "I won't be able to see a freakin' thing with a big mother like you in front of me."

BJ steadied the craft while Boris shifted to the front. "So you've been in one of these guys before?" Boris said, looking over his shoulder.

"Nah. But how hard can it be?"

They soon found out, nearly capsizing as BJ climbed in. The kayak was incredibly unstable. And when they finally managed to start paddling, they went around in a circle.

"Listen, Boris," BJ said, lifting his paddle out of the water. "You row on the starboard side. I'll row on the port."

"How come you get port?"

"Okay, you take port. I'll take starboard."

"Which is port?"

"You don't know?"

"You think I'm in the freakin' navy?"

BJ knew of port and starboard from books, but the truth was, he wasn't sure either. "Port's right," he guessed. "Starboard's left."

They set off, Boris paddling on the right, BJ on the left. But Boris's natural stroke was quick and jerky, while BJ's was slow and smooth, so their progress was fitful, and they ended up moving in a rightward arc. When they nearly hit a sailfish, BJ lifted his paddle again.

"Hey, man, we got to synchronize."

"What's that?" Boris said warily.

"Paddle in time with each other. I'll go faster, you go slower."

But that didn't work either. They still arced to the right.

"Maybe we got to shift back and forth," BJ said. "Maybe that's how come the paddles have the oar things on both ends. You start on port, I'll start on the starboard. Then we switch every stroke."

Though Boris complained bitterly when BJ splashed him, this approach worked better, and they managed to negotiate the channel that led from Portage Bay out to Lake Washington. On the lake the water soon turned choppy.

"We better go under the floating bridge while we can," BJ said.

"Why?"

"We're on the leeward side."

"What's that?"

"The side where the waves are. The other side's windward."

BJ wasn't sure about this terminology either, but Boris didn't challenge it. The floating bridge was on pontoons, so a boat could pass under it only near shore, where it rose up on stilts. Once they paddled through to the south side, the water was glassy, and as they got into a rhythm, BJ actually began to enjoy being out on the lake with the sun on his face. Boris seemed to enjoy it, too—till they'd been paddling about half an hour.

"This is whacked," he suddenly declared. "We should've ripped off that speedboat. My arms are about to fall off."

"It's good exercise."

"You got twenty pounds on me. I got to work that much harder."

"You're fourteen. I'm not even thirteen yet."

This shut Boris up. But the truth was BJ's arms were aching, too, and by the time they passed between the stilts on the east end of the bridge, he was thinking they should have taken the bus across the floating bridge and rented a kayak on this side.

All such regrets flew out of his head when they rounded Evergreen Point. "Wow," he said, gaping at the lakefront mansion he'd seen pictures of in magazines.

"How'd you like to have to mow that lawn!" Boris cried. "Look, tennis courts!"

"And check out the helipad!"

"Jeez, you could park a friggin' aircraft carrier at that dock. I don't see Nina, though."

"Or Darryl."

"Maybe they're inside beating each other's brains out at GameMaster."

As they paddled toward the dock, they clunked up against a log floating just beneath the water's surface, but the kayak bounced off it unharmed. They were still a good football field from the edge of the property when a Jet Ski swooshed up alongside them.

"Cove's private," barked the driver, a beefy man in a dark-red uniform, his eyes hidden by mirrored aviator glasses.

"We're visiting the Masterlys," BJ said.

"They expecting you?"

"Well, I'm a friend of Darryl Kirby. And this here's Nina Rizniak's brother."

"*Who?*"

"Darryl Kirby."

"And Nina Rizniak," Boris piped up.

"Never heard of them," the guard said.

"But . . . are you sure they don't live here?" BJ said.

"What are they? Gardeners? Housekeepers?"

"They're kids," BJ said. "Our age. I think Mr. Masterly adopted them. Can't we at least ask him?"

"Not if you don't have an appointment."

"But—"

"Sorry, boys. The Masterlys don't go in for sight-seers."

"But we paddled all the way across the friggin' lake!" Boris cried. "Can't we even rest on the dock a minute?"

"Like I said, it's private property."

Already red in the face from all the sun and exertion, Boris went almost purple.

"Let's go," BJ murmured, turning the bow of the kayak back out into the lake.

But Boris refused to do any paddling, and after a minute or two BJ stopped, too.

"I'm dying of thirst," Boris muttered.

"So am I."

"I'm hungry, too."

"Me, too."

Drifting along, they heard a roar and swiveled around. A boat sped out of the private cove, driven by another man in a dark-red uniform, pulling a water-skier who looked about eighteen, very tan, his sun-bleached hair whipping in the wind.

"It must be Keith Jr.," BJ said. "If he falls, maybe we could rescue him."

"He doesn't look like he's gonna fall, man."

Boris was right. The powerful boat and expert slalom skier shot past them. When they got out into the choppier water past the end of Evergreen Point, the boat looped back, the skier jumping the wake and sending arches of spray into the afternoon sunlight.

"When they come by, jump in and wave for help," BJ said. "He'll have to stop."

"Why me?"

"You're white. You'll stand out better against the water."

"No way, man."

"Come on, it's our only chance!"

"No way."

This time the boat nearly clipped the kayak, and they took on buckets of water. While they were bailing with their cupped hands, Boris cried: "Cripe, here it comes again!"

This time the ski boat gave them a wider berth. But as it shot by, the graceful skier plummeted headfirst into the water. He made hardly a splash, and the boat continued obliviously on, the handle of the ski rope skipping along between the wakes.

First the slalom ski popped up. A few seconds later the skier surfaced, floating facedown in the water. BJ and Boris paddled fiercely his way. When they reached him, BJ dropped his paddle and hauled the skier across the cockpit by his life vest. This nearly capsized the kayak, and sent Boris tumbling into the water, but BJ concentrated on the skier, administering a good smack on the back. The skier coughed and gagged and spat water, then slid off the kayak and started treading water, blinking up at BJ.

"What happened?" he asked.

"You took a header."

"Man, oh man. I hit a deadhead."

"A deadhead?"

"A log floating just below the surface. Skier's nightmare. Lucky you were here. Thanks a lot. I'm Kit."

"I'm BJ. This is . . ."

But there was no sign of Boris anywhere around the kayak. Alarmed, BJ slithered out of his cockpit into a lake far colder than at shallow Madison Beach. Icy as it was, he submerged his head and opened his eyes. A figure was flailing about four feet below him. BJ swam straight down to him—and Boris immediately got him in a death grip, leaving BJ no choice but to jab him in the solar plexus, causing what little air Boris had left to come shooting out of his mouth in bubbles. Though BJ was getting pretty desperate for air himself, he maneuvered behind Boris and grabbed his ponytail before frog-kicking back up to the surface.

BJ latched onto the kayak with one hand and pulled Boris's head above water with the other. Boris grabbed the front cockpit, his face squashed up against the fiberglass. He took a rattling breath, coughed up two or three cups of lake water, managed another breath, then sputtered and turned his head sideways so his cheek was against the kayak's hull. His eyeballs looked as if they were about to rupture.

"You come out in a kayak without a life vest," BJ cried, "and you can't even swim?"

"I'm drownded!" Boris croaked, spluttering.

"You're not drowned. You're just an idiot."

Boris was starting to catch his breath. "You almost pulled my hair out!" he said hoarsely.

"You're alive, aren't you?"

"You guys okay?" asked Kit, swimming around from

the other side of the kayak.

"I guess so," BJ said. "This idiot's Boris."

"Here, I'll hold this thing so you guys can get back in," Kit said.

Even with him bracing the kayak, getting back in was an adventure. By the time they managed it, the ski boat was roaring their way.

"Hey, Kit!" BJ cried over the rumble of the outboard. "Are you Keith Masterly's son?"

"That's right."

"Do you know Darryl Kirby?"

"Or Nina Rizniak?" Boris chimed in.

Kit shook his head. "Never heard of them. Sorry."

The driver cut the engine as the ski boat swooped up.

"Are you all right, sir?"

"Thanks to BJ and Boris here."

"I'm so sorry!" The driver put a ladder over the side of the boat. "I'd gotten used to you never falling."

"Don't worry about it." Kit climbed into the boat. "Ski's over there. Careful, there's a deadhead around here." He looked back down at the kayak. "Thanks, guys. Anything I can do for you?"

But the news that he'd never heard of Darryl or Nina was so discouraging that BJ just sighed and shook his head. Boris was even more dejected. Not only was there no Nina, his cigarettes, which he'd transferred from his sock to his shirt pocket, had gotten soaked. Only when the ski boat was out of earshot did it occur to either one of them that they could have asked to be pulled back across the lake.

## 22

The ruddy faces were blurry and wavery, but the eyes were all trained on him, filled with bitterness and recrimination. He inched closer, squinting, trying to make out who they were. Wasn't that his mother? And his father? Yes, and there was his brother! And his aunt and uncle and cousin! And his grandmother and grandfather! He reached out joyously toward his mother— and snatched his hand back, scalded.

"Rise and shine, friend and colleague. . . . "

Darryl sat bolt upright. He was in the luxurious bed in his rosy room in Paradise Lab. But although the sheets and pillowcases were as cool and crisp as ever, he was soaked with sweat.

Still shaky after showering, he changed into an ice-blue jumpsuit and hustled to the dining hall, where his vitamin awaited him by a glass of tomato juice at his place. Everything had changed since he'd skipped it yesterday. The rings had terrified him, and his room had been lonely, and now he was having nightmares.

Yet he hesitated to take the pale-blue pill. He didn't really want to forget about BJ and Mrs. Walker again.

And soon Nina came in and sat down beside him, which reminded him of the moon.

"To conquering Time!" Ruthie said, lifting her juice glass.

Darryl only pretended to pop the pill, instead squirreling it away in his pocket.

Down on L he ducked into Bio and studied his slide of G-17 until a hubbub lured him back out to the octagon. Mr. Masterly had returned to Paradise.

"Look, sir!" Paul Pettinio cried, waving a computer printout as he waddled up to the great man. "I've been changing the agitation rate on the compound."

Mr. Masterly glanced over the results. "This looks promising, Paul."

"Mr. Masterly!" Billy O'Connor cried from the doorway to Chem. "Come see! I've been building an armor for G-17 out of mercury!"

Though there was something creepy about the way they all clamored for Mr. Masterly's approval, Darryl couldn't help wishing *he* had an interesting finding or new idea to share.

After encouraging Greg Birtwissel's latest experiment with growth hormones, Mr. Masterly went to one of the computer stations and slipped a CD-ROM into the D drive. Everyone crowded around and watched a full-color model of the G-17 molecule bloom on the monitor.

"Thanks to groundwork laid by Suki and Mario," Mr. Masterly said, "the graphics department at MasterTech was able to complete this. Look how it shows all the ion permutations and hydrocarbon links."

Using the mouse, he moved the cursor to a circular icon on the tool bar and clicked. The entire complex molecule rotated slowly on its axis, giving them continuously different angles on its architecture.

"Wow," Darryl said, leaning in.

"Billy," Mr. Masterly said, "will you load the new image onto all the computers?"

"Yes, sir!" Billy cried.

Darryl spent the rest of that morning poring over the new image at one of the computers at the central console. It was far clearer than the real thing, and he was just reaching some interesting conclusions when a bell rang and the red globe lit up, revolving like the cherry on a police car.

"Who wants to take it?" Mr. Masterly said.

"Me!" came a chorus of three or four, Ruthie the loudest.

Darryl was trembling violently. As everyone else crowded around Ruthie, Nina tugged him out of his chair and dragged him into Bio.

"What's wrong?" she whispered, closing the door softly.

Darryl just stood there shuddering.

"Something really freaked you," she said. "If Mr. Masterly noticed, he'd know you're off the vitamin. Was it the bell? The red light?"

"Water," he managed.

She brought him a beaker of water from one of the sinks. He pulled the vitamin out of his pocket and popped it in his mouth.

"Don't!" Nina cried. "Throw it up!"

But he'd swallowed it. And in a matter of minutes he calmed down enough to return to his computer station.

## 23

Nina could have wrung his neck for taking the vitamin. But furious as she was, she was also curious. Why had he panicked like that? She spent the rest of the day watching Darryl go about his lab work and exercise and dinner in the same focused way as the rest of the team.

The next morning she was the first one in the dining hall. Hedderly had set the table, complete with glasses of pineapple juice and vitamins. She pocketed Darryl's tablet and sat down in chair number seven to wait for the others.

Darryl came in chattering with Billy O'Connor about the new G-17 image. They didn't stop talking about it until the food was served and Ruthie raised her glass "To conquering Time!"

"Give it to me," Darryl hissed.

Nina picked up her fork and sampled her poached egg.

"Thief," he whispered.

"Wuss," she whispered back.

A startled look crossed his face. His eyes fixed on his plate. Everyone else dug in, but he still hadn't so much as picked up his fork when the others got up to go.

"Come on, Darryl," Billy said, pulling him out of his chair. "There's this lecture on fission you've got to see."

Still looking dazed, Darryl followed Billy out of the dining hall. Nina wrapped the cinnamon roll he'd left on his plate in a napkin and followed them down to L. After spending half an hour with Billy in Video, Darryl ducked into Bio, and Nina went in and set the cinnamon roll by his microscope. He didn't thank her. He didn't speak to her at lunch, either. Or during exercise period, which he spent in the pool, never even glancing toward the gymnasium. Nor did he speak to her at dinner.

After dinner there was a general migration up to the AquaFilm, but Nina retreated to her room. She was lying in bed listening to "We'll Meet Again" when Darryl barged in.

"I want my vitamin," he said, crossing his arms over his chest in the doorway.

She sighed, swinging her legs over the side of the bed. "I didn't really mean you're a wuss, Darryl."

"I want my vitamin," he repeated.

"You just think you do. They make you feel better, but it's not real."

"So what? What's so wonderful about real? You like StarMaster, don't you? It's not real."

"But . . . facing things makes you stronger. Not a wuss."

He flinched.

"What is it, Darryl?"

"Nothing."

"No, what?"

He closed the door behind him and slumped down in one of the red velvet chairs. "Somebody used to call me that."

"Who?"

He said something, but too low to hear.

"Who?" she said, the last of her anger evaporated.

"My brother," he whispered. "Jason."

"What happened to him?"

Darryl lowered his eyes.

"Why did that bell bother you so much down on L? Or was it the flashing red light?"

He just kept studying the carpet.

"Darryl?"

He said nothing. She suddenly felt like going over and giving him a comforting hug, but she remained on the bed.

"Whatever it is," she said gently, "you ought to face up to it. Otherwise it'll make you its prisoner. Like you're a prisoner here."

He shot her a look. "Mr. Masterly said I could spend

the summer water-skiing if I wanted. Why would he say that if I was a prisoner?"

"He wanted you to think you had a choice."

"You mean . . . because he wants us to *want* to be here?"

"I figure orientation only works if you're psyched for the chemistry and stuff. It's like in this book about magic in my school library. It said nobody can hypnotize you if you don't want to be hypnotized. All that stuff about swaying a pocket watch in front of people's eyes and putting them in a trance is baloney."

"Did he mention talking with the dead?"

"Uh-huh. And you'd already taken a vitamin before you had the tour of Paradise, right? That's how it was with me."

"What made you stop taking it?"

"I dropped it one time at breakfast, like you did. Except mine rolled out behind my chair and Hedderly stepped on it. He pulverized it. I was scared to speak up. Then that night I started missing Boris something awful. I cried myself to sleep. But I decided I liked feeling lonely better than feeling numb."

"That sort of looks like Boris," Darryl said, eyeing the acrobat. "How'd you two get separated in that shelter?"

"Mr. Masterly said he'd be adopting Boris, too."

"Did you eat a pastry?"

"A lemon tart—in his private jet. Next thing I knew, I was right here."

"Do you remember orientation?"

"Not much. I figure they give you something that helps you absorb information but switches off the rest of your brain. The vitamins aren't so strong, but they still switch off parts of you. Not the parts that help you figure out the structure of G-17. Other parts."

"Like feelings."

"If you don't think about the past, or people you miss, you can concentrate better on isotopes and polymers."

"But, you know, Nina, I thought about G-17 today even after the vitamin started wearing off. It's pretty interesting. You think it'll ever really work? Rejuvenate DNA?"

"Maybe."

"It'll be like that DeathMaster game."

She sat up. "Is that why the red light bugged you?"

"What do you mean?"

"If you do well at DeathMaster on that Mondo thing, there's a red flash. I think it's taking your picture."

Darryl went pale.

"Is that it?" she said. "The red flash reminds you of being in the shelter?"

But instead of answering, Darryl just surveyed the room.

"Want to get out of this place?" he said.

"Of course. But if he was even a little bit worried about any of us escaping, do you think he'd leave a chest of diamonds lying around?"

"You'll have to go up your ventilation shaft."

"Oh, sure! It's got to be a hundred feet straight up."

"Chimney technique."

"What?"

"It's a rock-climbing thing. When there's long cracks in a rock face."

"How do you know about that?"

Again he didn't answer. Instead he asked the date.

"Um, August eighteenth, I think."

"You ought to go while the weather's still warm. In case you have to hike once you get out. You won't be able to carry any gear—and who knows where we are? When's Labor Day this year?"

"September fourth, I think."

"Shoot for that," he said. "It gives you a couple weeks to get in shape. You can train at night. Hedderly won't notice."

"I could never get up that shaft."

"Really? I thought you were a Flying Rizniak."

She couldn't help grinning at this. "Well, I guess I

could try. You may have to pull me up the last part, though."

He looked down at the carpet again.

"What?"

"I can't go."

"Why not?"

"I just can't. Unless I took a vitamin. And then I probably wouldn't care about escaping."

"But why?"

"Because," he muttered.

"Because why?"

"It's like you said. I'm a wuss."

## 24

**O**n the way back across Lake Washington, Boris rested as much as he rowed, but BJ never stopped paddling once. It was *his* bike and *his* wristwatch being held ransom at the rental shop. They made it back just before the place closed, and BJ was so exhausted by the whole ordeal that he barely made it through dinner that night.

He didn't wake till after ten the next morning, but once he was up, he wasted no time, wolfing down three bowls of cereal, hopping on his bike, and riding straight over to the shelter. When he slipped into the front hall, he heard voices coming from Ms. Grimsley's office, so he headed upstairs without bothering her. He found Boris smoking on the windowsill in the third-floor room.

"I thought your cigarettes got soaked."

"I copped a couple from the old bag in the kitchen. So what's your bright idea for today, Einstein?"

BJ pointed at the laptop on the desk.

"What about it?" Boris said.

"It's got to be the link."

"What link?"

"Between Darryl and your sister."

"Look, Masterly couldn't've adopted them. His own kid would know. My friggin' arms feel like spaghetti."

BJ sat down at the desk and booted up the laptop. As soon as he started negotiating the maze, Boris sidled over to watch.

"No, go right, yeah, go left there, no, not that way, dumb-dumb, there's a wall that way."

"Jeez, man, it's hard enough without you blowing smoke in my face."

But in spite of the smoke and the backseat driving BJ made it through. When the game list appeared, he clicked on StarMaster 3. Nothing happened for a while, but just as Boris went to flick his cigarette out the window, the question popped up:

**Want to play?**

BJ typed in:

**Yes.**

**Who are you?**

**BJ. You?**

**NABATW.**

"Hey," BJ said, looking over his shoulder. "What's your tattoo say?"

"What's it to you?" Boris said.

"Check this out."

Boris came back and peered at the screen. "You're pulling my chain."

"No, I'm not."

"Come on. You typed that in."

BJ typed in:

**I didn't get your name.**

The answer reappeared:

**NABATW.**

"No way!" Boris screeched. "That's Neen!"

"Your sister?"

"That's Neen! It's got to be!"

"What's it mean, NABATW?"

Before Boris could answer, the door opened.

"Mr. Walker," Ms. Grimsley said, frowning from the doorway. "I didn't know you were here."

"Just came by to visit Boris, ma'am."

Ms. Grimsley stepped in, sniffing the air. "Is that smoke?"

"Comes in the window from the kitchen," Boris said.

Ms. Grimsley didn't appear to buy this. "Come with me, Boris," she said, closing the laptop.

"Don't!" he cried, opening the laptop back up. "We're in the middle of a game."

"That can wait. There are some people downstairs who'd like to meet you."

"*Huh?*"

"Prospective foster parents. They're looking for a boy about your age. Their own son died in a boating accident."

"Then they don't want me! I can't even swim. Tell her, man."

"He can't swim," BJ said.

"That's neither here nor there," said Ms. Grimsley. "Let me smell your breath, Boris."

Boris turned away, but Ms. Grimsley took him by the shoulders and made him face her. "As I suspected. Brush your teeth and come join us in my office."

As soon as she left, hands gripped BJ's shoulders like vices. "Get her back!"

The screen had gone blank, and when BJ hit "Enter," another maze appeared.

"Crud," he said.

"Go through it! Come on!"

But this time BJ was two or three turnings away from the exit when the two minutes elapsed.

"Try again!" Boris cried. "That was Neen!"

But again BJ failed. And before he could make another stab at it, Ms. Grimsley came back and shepherded them impatiently out of the room.

## 25

**D**arryl came home from a field trip to the Pacific Science Center to find the house deserted. Or so it seemed. When he went up to his room, there was Jason, sound asleep in bed, even though it wasn't dark out yet.

"What's going on?"

Jason didn't stir, so Darryl went to check his parents' room. They were sound asleep, too!

"Are you guys sick?"

Neither of them answered or even rolled over. He crept up to the bedside and felt his mother's forehead to see if she had a temperature.

"Ow!" he cried, yanking his hand away. "You're on fire!"

"Rise and shine, friend and colleague. . . ."

Darryl jerked up. He wasn't in his parents' bedroom, he was in his fancy bedroom in Paradise Lab. His whole body was trembling, and his hand still tingled as if it really had been scalded.

But a nice long shower calmed him down, and later, down on L, he put the bad dream out of his mind by concentrating on the new G-17 image on a computer in a carrel in Books, where he was safe from the flashing red light. The more he scrutinized the molecule, the more determined he became to stabilize it. He'd never been really and truly baffled before, not by the most ticklish math problems in CastleMaster, not by the Individualists' wiliest brainteasers in StarMaster 3.

He became so absorbed that he didn't realize he was no longer alone till he felt hands on his shoulders.

"It's lunchtime, Darryl."

"Mr. Masterly!"

"You like our new image?"

Darryl wanted to squirm away from the man, but at the same time he wanted to impress him. "It's fantastic, sir. You can see the molecular scaffolding so clearly."

"Has it given you any bright ideas?"

"Actually, yeah."

"What would that be?"

"Chopping it in two."

Mr. Masterly laughed. "Seriously."

"But there's a natural division." Darryl broke the image up into two pieces. "G-$9^{1/2}$ and G-$7^{1/2}$. They remain bonded, but when they're cleaved, they're stronger. I think we could do it in the accelerator."

Mr. Masterly leaned closer to the monitor, intrigued. "Divide and conquer, eh?"

It was Nina's day for lunchtime game duty, so

instead of talking with her in undertones while he ate, Darryl pondered G-9$\frac{1}{2}$ and G-7$\frac{1}{2}$. When he got back down to L, Nina was sharing a sandwich with Snoodles at the computer console.

"How's it going?" Darryl said.

"Well, we had a player. But only for a second."

He eyed the red light warily. "Rosalie_W again?"

"No, she called herself BJ. Or he."

"BJ?"

"Yeah."

"Are you all r-r-right, young s-s-sir?"

Darryl blinked from the young face to the old one. "I have a friend called BJ."

"Is he in a Masterly shelter?" Nina asked.

"No. But he delivers library books to one."

It was a wasted afternoon for Darryl. He huddled safely in Books, yet he listened so intently for the bell that he barely focused on G-17. If BJ got through again, he *had* to be the one to play him.

But the bell never rang.

In the dining room that evening the team was just starting their main course when Mr. Masterly's voice came over the PA system:

"When you're finished eating, Darryl, I could use you down on L."

Darryl felt all eyes on him. Though Nina looked

worried, everyone else looked kind of jealous, and despite last night's conversation he couldn't help feeling pleased at being singled out this way.

Down on L, Snoodles had just harvested a fresh blue freckle from a newly mixed batch of G-17. Mr. Masterly took it into Accel and invited Darryl to join him there.

"What do you think?" he said. "Gamma rays?"

Darryl thought for a minute and shook his head. "I'd bombard it with beta rays, sir. Should be cleaner."

He was right. In an hour they had several cc's of G-$9^{1/2}$ and several cc's of G-$7^{1/2}$.

"What dilution?" Mr. Masterly asked.

"I'd say about ten to one, sir."

"Saline solution?"

"Mm."

After diluting the new compound, Mr. Masterly went into Bio and set four cages, each containing a crusty old white rat, on the central table. He left one rat alone, as a control, and injected the other three with the newly split G-17. The rats weren't particularly cooperative, so it was well after nine o'clock before Darryl got back up to S.

"Come in," Nina said when he knocked on her door.

Sitting up in bed, still fully dressed, she paused her movie as he plunked down in one of the velvet chairs. But she didn't speak.

"He wanted help," Darryl said.

"Doing what?"

"Dividing G-17. What are you watching?"

"*Big Night under the Big Top.* Dividing it?"

"Just an idea of mine."

"What happened to training for the chimney climb?"

"I'm sorry. We could start tomorrow. But . . . Nina?"

"Yeah?"

"BJ's the one I wanted to call the other night. He and his mom were so great to me. If he gets through again, will you tell him where I am?"

"You think I know where we are?"

"You know what I mean. Tell him we're in this place where we can't call out."

"Oh. Okay, I guess."

"And you'll do lunch duty tomorrow?"

"Uh-uh. It's against the rules to do two days in a row."

Darryl sighed, looking down at the carpet.

"What's wrong?"

"Mr. Masterly's leaving tonight. He's got a meeting at MasterTech in the morning. But he said he'd be back by lunchtime, and I bet he goes straight to L to check the rats."

"What rats?"

"We injected some rats."

"So?"

"I can't do lunch duty."

"Because you'll freeze up if the red light comes on?"

"And he'll know I'm off the vitamins."

"Then you better not freeze up."

"I can't help it."

"Why does the flashing red light bug you so much?"

But letting his mind slide off in that direction was too dangerous. So he just sat there like a lump.

Suddenly Nina was kneeling before him, her eyes peering into his through the thick lenses of her glasses. "Tell me, Darryl," she said.

When he still didn't speak, she took his hands.

"Tell me."

It felt funny, her holding his hands. Hers were kind of hard, callused from gymnastics, but they were nice and warm. He swallowed.

"It's all my fault," he said.

"What's all your fault?"

When he didn't answer again, she let go of him and went into the bathroom and returned with a glass of water. He took a drink.

"Thanks," he said.

She knelt down and took his hands again. "Now tell me." She smiled at him. "Come on, Darryl. Don't be a wuss."

Darryl's heart felt like one of those rats trying to

avoid the needle. "That's just what he used to say," he whispered.

"Your brother Jason?"

Darryl nodded. "He said it . . . that night."

"What night?"

Darryl opened his mouth, but no words came out.

"Come on, Darryl," Nina coaxed. "Tell me. Tell me about that night."

## 26

"**W**hy do you always have to be such a wuss, Dare? It gets embarrassing being your brother."

"I'm not a wuss."

"Go on, Dare, it's fun. I'd sleep up there with you if I could get up the darn ladder."

The three boys were lounging around the living room of their grandparents' house after a chicken-pot-pie dinner. Darryl was in his grandfather's easy chair. His brother, Jason, was sprawled on the sofa where Darryl had slept the night before. Their cousin Barry, who was eighteen, a year older than Jason, was sprawled on the other sofa, his leg in a cast. He'd wrapped his parents' Subaru around a streetlamp the night of his senior prom.

"The only bad thing about that tree hut's the darn birds," Barry said. "They start hootin' and hollerin' at about five A.M."

"Dare won't mind that," Jason said. "He's used to that nerdy GameMaster, blippin' and beepin' all the time."

"It's not nerdy," Darryl muttered. "If you ask me, you're the wuss. Scared of Old Man Truman's ghost."

"Yeah, right," Jason said with a snort. "I just want to

get a decent night's sleep, that's all."

"But this morning you said you liked the tree hut."

Jason yawned. "I don't know about you, Barry, but I'm about ready to hit the hay."

"It's not fair!" Darryl cried.

"What's all the ruckus in there?" Uncle Frank called from the front porch.

"Just Dare being a wuss, as usual," Jason called back.

Darryl heard the screen door and the creaking floorboards but couldn't see who'd come inside till his plump aunt and even plumper uncle entered the glow of the kerosene lantern set on the mantelpiece under the needlepoint Kirby Family Tree. They'd all ferried over here from Seattle the day before to celebrate his grandmother's sixty-fifth birthday: he and Jason and their parents and Barry and his parents. His grandparents had retired to Bainbridge Island a couple of years ago, buying a house from a family that had outgrown it. There were only three bedrooms, and last night Darryl had camped out in the living room with Barry while Jason had slept in the tree hut built by the previous owners' kids. This afternoon a freak windstorm had swept up Puget Sound and knocked out the electricity, so tonight their only light was lanterns and candles. If Darryl had had his way, the storm would have knocked down the sycamore in the backyard with the tree hut in it—but no such luck.

"Can't you kids keep it down to a dull roar?" Uncle Frank said. "Granny and Gramps are sleeping."

"Sorry, Pop," said Barry.

The screen door squeaked again, and Darryl's parents entered the circle of flickering light. They weren't a bit plump. There wasn't an ounce of body fat on either one of them.

"What's the problem?" Mr. Kirby asked.

"Dare doesn't want to sleep in the tree hut, Dad," Jason said.

"Why not?"

"It's all your doing, Martin," Aunt Ellie said to Darryl's father. "Your ghost story's got them scared to sleep outdoors."

"How could I resist, with the candles throwing all those shadows on the walls?"

"I'm not scared of Old Man Truman's ghost," Jason said.

At dinner Mr. Kirby had described a ghost that supposedly haunted parties of hikers on Mount St. Helens. An old man named Truman had refused to evacuate his cabin on the side of the mountain when it blew its stack back in 1979, so he'd ended up buried in ash and lava.

"I just feel like being comfortable tonight," Jason said. "Is that a crime?"

"Well, I guess it's your turn," Mrs. Kirby said. "What's the problem, Dare?"

"He said he *liked* the tree hut, Mom," Darryl said.

"So? Now it's your turn to like it."

"But I don't want to."

"Oh, for cripe's sake," Mr. Kirby said.

Darryl felt a hand on his shoulder: Aunt Ellie's. "Don't be hard on him, Martin. His only problem's his brains. Super-smart people worry about things like ghosts."

"I'm not scared of ghosts," Darryl protested.

"Then what are you worried about, hon?" Mrs. Kirby said. "You're not going to get hypothermia in July."

"The boy genius is scared of heights," Jason said. "Simple as that."

"Good grief, it's not even twenty feet up," Mrs. Kirby said. "And the tree hut's got a door—you can't fall out."

"If you don't want to go up in that tree, Dare," Aunt Ellie said, "we can put the two armchairs together and make you a bed."

"Good lord," Mr. Kirby said. "Most kids'd kill for a chance to sleep in a tree hut."

At this Darryl marched indignantly into the kitchen and banged out the back door. But one look at the backyard sycamore turned his indignation to foreboding. The windstorm had scoured the sky clean, and the tree was silhouetted against a field of stars thicker than the one on the opening screen of StarMaster 2. As his mother had said, the tree hut, which looked like a big wooden crate wedged where three limbs came together, couldn't have been more than twenty feet off the ground. But as his brother had said, Darryl was scared of heights. Had been since the Space Needle incident. It just wasn't something you advertised when your parents were rock climbers.

A ladder of crooked slats was nailed to the trunk. Darryl climbed it with gritted teeth and threw himself into the tree hut. He shut the door behind him and huddled in a corner, shaking like a leaf. Shaking far more violently, in fact, than the leaves out the window, for in the wake of the storm there wasn't a breath of wind. He pulled off his sweatshirt and pants and stuffed them in the window so he wouldn't have to look out; then he curled up in the sleeping bag his brother had left there.

"I wish you were all dead," Darryl muttered, hugging himself. "I wish you were all dead. . . ."

He woke to a strange crackling sound, like someone grinding ice. It didn't smell like ice though. He sat up and, steeling himself for the dizzying view, pulled his wadded clothes out of the window.

A few yards away, a red light was swirling on the cab of a fire engine.

## 27

**W**hen Darryl got to this point in his story, it felt as if somebody was tightening a noose around his throat. He lost his voice entirely. And that wasn't the worst. A tear slipped out of his left eye.

He turned and faked a cough, trying to wipe his face without Nina noticing. Then a tear squirted out of his right eye. Followed quickly by another. Then his left eye starting leaking again.

He jerked to his feet. He had to get out of there. But now the tears were pouring out so furiously that all he could see was a fiery blur.

As he groped toward the door, he heard the swoosh of the wall panel. Before he could escape, Nina took his arm and guided him back to the chair and pushed him down and set a box of tissues in his lap.

"Go on, Darryl, cry. It's good for you."

He covered his face, humiliated.

"You lost your whole family." From her voice it sounded as if she was kneeling at his feet again. "I only lost my mom, and I cried for weeks."

A sob broke out of him—and, just like that, his

resistance melted. He simply started sobbing. He sobbed for his mother, and his father, and his aunt Ellie. He sobbed for his grandparents and his uncle and cousin and even his brother. He sobbed for ten minutes, twenty minutes, half an hour, sobbing and sobbing and sobbing till his gut ached so much, he had to curl up in the chair like a baby.

He'd gone through the whole box of tissues—and lost enough saline solution to dilute a full beaker of G-17—before his tear ducts finally dried up. Uncoiling himself, he blinked down at Nina, a human island surrounded by a flotilla of wadded-up tissues. She got up and went into the bathroom and returned with another glass of water.

Drinking it loosened the noose a little.

"Sorry I'm such a wuss," he said in a croaky voice.

"You're not a wuss."

Over the next couple of hours she gently prodded him for the rest of the story, and he told her bits and pieces about the ashy skeleton of his grandparents' house and his numb night in the police station on Bainbridge Island and his numb ferry ride back to Seattle and his numb visit to a hospital near his house and his numb first week at the Masterly Children's Shelter. It was close to dawn when exhaustion finally overcame them.

"Rise and shine . . ."

Blinking groggily in the brightening light, Darryl saw that he was still in one of the red velvet chairs in Nina's room, while Nina was curled up on the floor amid the crumpled tissues. Her glasses had fallen off, but she found them and blinked at him as the pep talk petered out.

"Are you okay?"

"I'm really tired."

"Me, too. Maybe we can say we're sick and sleep in."

"Yeah . . . no!"

He jumped up.

"What is it?"

"What if BJ gets through again?"

## 28

When BJ slipped in through the shelter's front door, he was surprised to spot Boris among the kids eating lunch in the dining room. He'd last seen him the day before, being led into the office by Ms. Grimsley, and he'd figured that if the prospective foster parents hadn't taken him, Boris would have skedaddled. Ms. Grimsley was eating lunch, too, her back to BJ, so he tiptoed across the Oriental rug and scooted up the front stairs unseen. Or so he thought. He'd just walked into the third-floor room when Boris popped in after him.

"Thought that was you. You'd make a sad-ass burglar."

"We can't all be born sneaks," BJ said, noting that the old leather suitcase and Boris's backpack and the toolbox were all under one of the beds. "How'd it go with the foster parents?"

Boris reached under the bed and pulled a cigarette out of a pouch in his pack, then moved to the open window for his after-lunch smoke. "Grimface says I scared them off," he said, exhaling into the madrona tree.

"How'd you do that?"

He sniggered. "It was you, bud. They had some file

on me and saw my birthday's next month and asked what I wanted. I said how somebody kiped my switchblade and I wanted a new one."

BJ cracked a smile.

"I spent all morning trying to get through that stupid maze," Boris said, narrowing his eyes at the laptop.

It was on. BJ sat at the desk and hit the Enter key. "Don't start blowing smoke in my face," he warned when the maze appeared.

As BJ studied it, Boris, minus his cigarette, came and stood behind him.

"Come on, man. You only got ninety seconds to go."

But BJ was using Darryl's technique of visualizing the entire path before starting. He didn't move the little figure till there was less than a minute left, and he made it through with three seconds to spare.

"Beege rules!" Boris cried, clapping him on the back.

The words

**Want to play?**

appeared on the screen. BJ typed:

**Yes. Who are you?**

**MDK. Who are you?**

"Crud," Boris said. "No Neen."
BJ typed:

**BJ.**

**BJ Walker?**

Breathless, BJ typed:

**Is that Darryl Kirby?**

**Yes!**

"I can't believe it," BJ said in a choked voice.
"Ask him about Neen!" Boris cried.
BJ typed:

**Where in the world are you?**

**Paradise Lab. It's somewhere in Washington
State, that's all I know. There's no telephones.
That's why I haven't called.**

**Are you okay?**

**I'm alive. Where are you?**

**The shelter. What's Paradise Lab?**

**Keith Masterly's special think tank. You can't get out. They drug you and make you work on G-17.**

"We were right!" BJ said. "It *was* Keith Masterly!"
"Come on!" Boris cried, shaking BJ's shoulders. "Ask if Neen's there!"

**Is Nina there?**

**Yes. She's my friend.**

**What do you mean by G-17?**

**Uh-oh, he's coming.**

**Who?**

But instead of an answer, the opening screen for StarMaster 3 flashed up on the monitor.

## 29

**M**r. Masterly stepped out of the elevator and strode over to the computer console.

"Got a nibble?" he asked.

"I think s-so," said Snoodles, who'd been eating lunch with Darryl.

"You look excited, Darryl. Somebody smart?"

Darryl was vibrating like a tuning fork. He'd volunteered for lunch duty, and when the flashing red light came on, he miraculously hadn't frozen up. And now he'd gotten through to BJ!

"He doesn't look too good," Mr. Masterly said. "He's not even hunting for star gates. Probably got lucky with the maze."

"But we just started, sir."

After watching a while, Mr. Masterly clucked his tongue. "Why are you toying with him like that? For heaven's sake, he hasn't recruited a single Individualist. Finish him off and come with me."

In spite of everything Darryl had been disappointed when he'd gone into Bio that morning and found the three injected rats as old and crusty as the uninjected one. But all that seemed meaningless now that he'd contacted BJ.

"You better go look at the rats, sir. I don't think it worked."

"Damn. I thought you might be onto something. Here, let me."

Mr. Masterly took over the keyboard and finished BJ off in short order. Only then did he go into Bio.

Darryl remained at the computer, hoping against hope that the red light he'd so feared yesterday would come on again. But it never did.

At Nina's suggestion they both skipped gym period that day in favor of naps. After dinner they napped again, and later, once the rest of the team went to bed, they crept up the emergency stairs to E, put on their cross-training shoes, and crept back down to S. Hedderly was chopping celery for tomorrow's soup when they walked into the kitchen.

"Midnight snacking, kiddos?" he said.

"Yup," they answered.

They slipped into the pantry, pulled off the vent cover, and slid in. Darryl had hoped that his fear of heights might have dissolved along with his fear of flashing red lights, but the bottom dropped out of his stomach when he peered up the dizzying tube.

"So what's this chimney thing?" Nina whispered.

The chimney technique was meant for climbing vertical rock chutes and involved pressing the back against one side of a shaft and the hands and feet and even the knees against the other. Using one hand to keep from slipping down, the climber used the other hand and both feet to inch himself upward. Darryl's parents had made it look easy, but he now learned what a tiring method of climbing it was. The Teflon shaft was slick, too, and that first night neither he nor Nina made it beyond the place where the stove vent merged.

The next night they did a little better, and the night after that a little better yet. But the fourth night they couldn't train at all, for when they got to the shaft, water was trickling down it, making it perilously slippery.

"It must be raining out in the world," Nina said wistfully.

"I always complained about Seattle weather," Darryl said. "Now I'd love to feel some rain on my face."

"Why do you think there's no cap up there to keep the rain out?"

"Maybe we're way underground and he doesn't want somebody walking by up there to notice anything."

"But somebody might fall in. They'd notice that."

They couldn't explain why the top should be open, but the next night the vent was dry, and they both made it up to a seam that allowed them to catch their breath.

There turned out to be seams every ten feet or so, making good rest stops. After a week Nina reached the third seam—about thirty percent of the way out. Physically, Darryl probably could have reached the third seam, too, but even though he made a point of never looking back down the shaft, the whirring in his gut got so bad by the second seam that instead of going higher, he climbed back down to the first seam and then back up again. On the night of their escape, he would just have to suck it up.

Mr. Masterly had been popping in and out of Paradise Lab in his usual unpredictable way, but one evening at dinner toward the end of August he announced over the PA that he would be gone for a full week to help launch a new division of MasterTech. After the meal, when Darryl went back to room eight to rest up for that night's training, he found a note on his pillow.

*Darryl—*
*I still believe you were onto something. Keep thinking.*
                                                          *—KM*

Flattered in spite of himself, Darryl spent the next day studying the computer-generated image of G-17. He ran the molecule through X-ray crystallography and pored over the results. Over those next few days he became convinced that the reason for his failure was the breakdown of the G-9$^{1}/_{2}$ molecule. He finally concluded that G-17 had two natural divisions, not just one. On the Thursday before Labor Day he got Snoodles to whip him up a fresh blue freckle and spent the morning in Accel dividing it. That afternoon he subdivided G-9$^{1}/_{2}$ into G5 and G-4$^{1}/_{2}$; then he diluted the entire new compound and injected some into one of the crusty old rats.

There turned out to be seams every ten feet or so, making good rest stops. After a week Nina reached the third seam—about thirty percent of the way out. Physically, Darryl probably could have reached the third seam, too, but even though he made a point of never looking back down the shaft, the whirring in his gut got so bad by the second seam that instead of going higher, he climbed back down to the first seam and then back up again. On the night of their escape, he would just have to suck it up.

Mr. Masterly had been popping in and out of Paradise Lab in his usual unpredictable way, but one evening at dinner toward the end of August he announced over the PA that he would be gone for a full week to help launch a new division of MasterTech. After the meal, when Darryl went back to room eight to rest up for that night's training, he found a note on his pillow.

*Darryl—*
*I still believe you were onto something. Keep thinking.*
                                                        *—KM*

Flattered in spite of himself, Darryl spent the next day studying the computer-generated image of G-17. He ran the molecule through X-ray crystallography and pored over the results. Over those next few days he became convinced that the reason for his failure was the breakdown of the G-$9\frac{1}{2}$ molecule. He finally concluded that G-17 had two natural divisions, not just one. On the Thursday before Labor Day he got Snoodles to whip him up a fresh blue freckle and spent the morning in Accel dividing it. That afternoon he subdivided G-$9\frac{1}{2}$ into G5 and G-$4\frac{1}{2}$; then he diluted the entire new compound and injected some into one of the crusty old rats.

## 30

**B**oris had spent that same week sleeping in the bottom bunk in the Walkers' basement. It had struck BJ that two heads would be better than one in solving the mystery of Paradise Lab—and as for his mother, the story of Boris losing his sister had naturally melted her heart. Boris grumbled about BJ's no-smoking-in-the-house policy, but otherwise the two boys had been getting on surprisingly well—probably because they hadn't spent much time together. After coming up blank in an internet search for Paradise Lab, they'd started canvassing Seattle area laboratories, and there were so many, they'd had to split up.

By the time BJ walked out of Capitol Hill Laboratories that Thursday afternoon, he'd come up empty for the ninth straight time. There didn't seem to be a lab worker in the city who'd so much as heard of a Paradise Lab. He shuffled home up Pike Street feeling pretty discouraged—until he got to Capitol Hill Mercedes. As he peered in at the spanking-new models on the showroom floor, a woman's voice echoed in his head:

*"But didn't he report the car missing to you? It is an S-GPS Special."*

BJ was decently dressed for his lab visits, so when he went in to inspect the cars, the salesman, a balding man in a brown suit, was reasonably polite. BJ told him that his mother was thinking of buying his father a Mercedes for their twenty-fifth wedding anniversary.

"She's kind of dumb about cars, so she asked me to stop in. Do you have one of those S-GPS 600's?"

The salesman looked doubtful but led him over to a sleek burgundy sedan with a mushroom interior. "Is your mother aware of the sticker price?" he asked, pointing to the specs sheet on the back window.

"Oh, money's no problem," BJ said breezily. "Both my folks are execs at MasterTech."

"Would you like me to take you on a test drive?" the salesman said, suddenly perking up. "You won't believe how smooth and quiet she runs."

"That's okay, I've ridden in all kinds of Mercedes—everyone on our street has one. I was just curious about the S-GPS stuff. What's it mean exactly?"

"GPS means Global Positioning System. Take a look."

The salesman opened the driver's side door for him, and in spite of his vast experience with fancy cars, BJ was amazed by the rich smell of the leather bucket seats and the dashboard's resemblance to the instrument panel on the shuttle craft in which Captain Geomopolis escapes the conspirators who take over his starship in *Star Voyager*.

The salesman got in the passenger side. "The GPS works without the ignition," he said, pressing a button on what looked like a little TV set mounted below the radio and CD player. A map of the Capitol Hill area appeared on the screen, with a pulsing dot marking their location. "If you're in a strange city, you can find your way anywhere." He pressed the button again, and the map changed to all of Seattle, with the pulsing dot still indicating their position. He pressed it again and the map became all of western Washington State. Then the whole state. Then the entire western United States, a pulse showing in Seattle, in the northwest corner. "And here's the special feature," he said, opening the glove compartment. "Your personal tracker."

The personal tracker was a little bigger than a cell phone, a little smaller than a GameMaster. The salesman flipped open the screen and pressed a button. A map of Capitol Hill appeared on the tracker, complete with pulsing dot.

"You carry this in your pocket or briefcase and it always shows where the car is. So if it's lost or stolen, you can locate it instantly. It's becoming a popular feature."

The salesman gave BJ a brochure describing all the car's luxuries, and BJ left him with the assurance that he would be back soon with his mother. However, he neglected to mention his visit to the dealership to his mother that evening at dinner.

After dinner he and Boris adjourned to the basement to compare notes on their days.

"This one guy at this lab on Western knew about a Paradise *Club*," Boris said. "But he said it's a stripper joint. How'd you do?"

BJ just grinned.

"What, man? You come up with something?"

"An idea."

"What?"

He told him about the Global Positioning System. "We could stash one in Masterly's helicopter. That way we can track where it goes. It'll be just like in *Star Voyager*."

"Huh?"

"The movie. You've seen it, right?"

"Uh-uh."

"You've never seen *Star Voyager?*" BJ said incredulously.

"You think my old man gave us movie money?"

"It was on TV. Twice."

"So? It's one of them outer space things, right? I go for bank heists and prison breaks, stuff like that."

"There's this great part where Captain Geomopolis sends a cyborg on a suicide mission to stick a magnetic detector on the outside of a—"

"That's just what I mean. Sci-fi's whacked. How can you send a cyborg on a freakin' suicide mission? They ain't even alive. They're just nuts and bolts. How can they commit suicide?"

BJ heaved an exasperated sigh. "I only mean 'suicide mission' in the . . . in the . . ."

"In the what?"

"Listen, the point is the magnetic detector. It's the same principle."

"That right? Ours was this old bat with a face like a Salisbury steak."

"What?"

"Salisbury steak. It's this crud they give you at the shelter. It's like the worst cut of meat you can get, so they pound the crap out of it so it won't be so tough, except it doesn't work. It's got these stringy things that get caught in your teeth."

"I don't know what you're talking about," BJ said, bewildered.

"Mrs. Crushmeier. Our old principal."

"I didn't mean school principal, I meant the same principle, like . . . the same idea. They put this magnetic detector on the starship so they can track it right through the meteor shower. Same idea as putting the GPS in the helicopter."

"Right, and real life's just like the movies."

"I don't see why it shouldn't work. We could borrow Grimface's. We'll go up to the shelter in the morning with your toolbox. The GPS is in the car, and the personal tracker's probably in her handbag."

The corners of Boris's mouth turned up. "Ripping off Grimface, eh? But even if we get the thingamajig, how do we get it in Masterly's helicopter?"

"We put it there."

"How?"

"We saved Keith Jr.'s life, didn't we? You think he won't give us lunch and a tour of the place if we show up?"

"You think?"

"What do we have to lose from trying? Unless you've got a better idea."

"Me? How am I supposed to think when I can't smoke?"

## 31

**W**hen the two boys got to the shelter the next morning, the sky was the same steely gray as Ms. Grimsley's hair, but at least it wasn't raining, and a bunch of the orphans were playing football on the side lawn. One thing BJ and Boris had managed to agree on was that BJ had better people skills and Boris had better burglar skills. So Boris remained crouched in the rhododendrons with his toolbox while BJ walked into the Shelter.

The office door was ajar. BJ opened it wider and said:

"Morning, Ms. Grimsley."

Ms. Grimsley looked up from some paperwork on her desk. "It's not Saturday, is it?" she said. "If you're here to visit Mr. Rizniak, we haven't seen hide nor hair of him in over a week."

"I'm just looking for a book that's overdue."

"What book?"

"Um, it's called *Paradise Lab*."

If the name meant anything to her, she certainly didn't show it. As for her own paperback, she wasn't reading it today, but her handbag was hanging off the back of her chair as usual.

"Are the kids in their rooms?" BJ asked.

"I think most of them are outside playing."

Though BJ knew this, he drifted over to the window anyway. "Yeah, you're right," he said, flicking open the lock on top of the sash before turning back. "Could you help me find it? Ma says three people have it on reserve at the library."

Ms. Grimsley reluctantly got up. On the second floor they went from room to room, BJ making an elaborate show of hunting for the fictitious book. By the time they got up to the third floor, Ms. Grimsley's patience was fraying.

"It can't be in here," she said, following BJ into the familiar room with the ruddy-barked tree out the window. "The only person who's used this lately is Boris, and he's certainly no reader."

Nevertheless BJ looked under the beds and behind the curtains. The last straw was when he opened the window and leaned out.

"Squirrels didn't steal it, for heaven's sake! Come on, young man, I've got a lot on my plate today."

BJ could see Boris's legs disappearing through the office window two stories below. Ms. Grimsley came over and tugged his arm.

"This is ridiculous," she said, closing the sash.

BJ traipsed downstairs in her wake. On the lower staircase he moaned and plopped down on one of the carpeted steps.

"What in the world?"

He winced, massaging his left ankle. "I think I twisted something, ma'am."

"Is this some sort of setup? If you have ideas of suing us, I'd advise you to think again. Mr. Masterly has an entire law firm at his beck and call."

"I sprained something. Honest."

"Can you stand up?"

As he pulled himself slowly to his feet, he peered over the banister. A hand appeared in the office door-way, thumb up.

"Okay, lean on me," Ms. Grimsley said grudgingly, positioning herself beside him.

He put just enough weight on her bony shoulder to be convincing.

"Well, I suppose I'll have to run you home," she said when they reached the foot of the stairs. "Wait here— I'll get my car keys."

"No!"

"No?"

BJ tested his ankle. "It's better."

"Already?"

"It must have been that darned pinched nerve. Skateboard injury. It acts up sometimes. But I appreciate the offer, Ms. Grimsley."

He turned and fake-limped out of the shelter. As he crossed the gravel circle, he didn't so much as glance toward the garage. He didn't look at the kids playing football, either. Eyes straight ahead, he limped down the driveway and turned right.

He and Boris had agreed to rendezvous at the 7-Eleven two blocks west of the shelter. BJ waited in front of the store till the pimply guy at the front register started shooting him dirty looks through the glass doors, at which point he moved over by a Dumpster in the side parking lot. The sky was looking more and more ominous, and with each passing minute he got more and more agitated, till he was as jumpy as one of Quadros's fleas. But just when he was about to head back to the shelter, a scrawny, ponytailed figure ambled into the parking lot.

BJ had worn good clothes and insisted Boris wear his new hand-me-downs, but the knees of Boris's khakis were now stained and there was a rip in his shirt sleeve.

"How'd it go, man?"

"Piece of cake."

Boris swiveled around, and BJ unzipped his pack.

"Way to go!" BJ said, seeing a GPS and a personal tracker like the ones in the showroom car.

"Lucky they don't make a personal tracker for the personal tracker, huh?"

"What's this?" BJ asked, pulling out a paperback.

"That was in her bag, too. Looked kinda juicy."

On the cover a brutish man with wavy, raven-black hair was holding a delicate blond captive in his arms.

"She's probably missed it already," BJ said, tossing it back into the pack. "We better get out of here."

"Not till I get some cigs. Give me a five, willya?"

Boris had seen BJ extract his GameMaster savings, a wad of over a hundred dollars, from his strongbox in the bottom of his fridge/closet that morning. But BJ didn't even acknowledge the request, simply heading for the pay phone at the Exxon station across the street.

When he got back to the Dumpster, there was no sign of Boris. But Boris soon came sauntering out of the 7-Eleven and lit up a cigarette.

"Jeez, man, we got to lie low," BJ hissed when he got to the Dumpster. "Did you take money out of Grimface's wallet?"

"Not all of it," Boris said, gatling out a series of small smoke rings.

"And that guy in the store sold to you?"

"I gave him a tip. Hope he uses it to buy some zit cream."

As a squad car pulled into the station, BJ yanked Boris behind the Dumpster. Peeking out, he watched a policewoman walk into the store and emerge with a Styrofoam cup. She set it on the hood of her car and strode straight over to the Dumpster.

"I *thought* I saw smoke. Aren't you a little young for that?"

"I'm older than I look," Boris muttered, dropping his cigarette and grinding it out on the pavement.

"Must've stunted your growth. What are you boys up to?"

Luckily the cab BJ had called pulled into the parking lot at that very moment.

"Heading home, officer," BJ said. "That's ours."

**32**

The cabdriver had a turban on his head and a scary-looking scar on his cheek, but his voice, high-pitched and singsongy, wasn't the least bit scary.

"Hunt Point?" he said, craning his head around to look at the boys in the backseat. "Hunt Point way across lake. You got twenty dollar?"

BJ yanked out his wad, whereupon the driver put the cab in gear.

Once they were on the floating bridge, BJ pulled the GPS out of Boris's pack.

"Piece of cake?" he said, noting a sizeable dent in the top.

"It had these weird screws that don't screw," Boris confessed. "I had to get the crowbar out of the trunk and give it a little help."

"Nobody saw you?"

"Guess not."

"What happened to the toolbox?"

"I ditched it under a bush on my way out. Figured we didn't need it anymore."

BJ pushed a button—and a map of Lake Washington

instantly appeared on the screen, Seattle on the west side, Bellevue on the east. A pulsing dot was crawling like an ant across the bridge connecting the two cities. When the pulsing dot, and the taxi, reached the east side of the lake, the cab, and the dot, took the Hunt's Point exit. BJ had the driver head up Hunt's Point Road.

BJ rolled down his window as they pulled up to the guardhouse. "BJ and Boris to see Kit," he told the mustachioed guard.

The guard looked dubious as he ducked into the guardhouse, but when he emerged, he touched his cap politely and raised the gate. As the cab started up a curving driveway, the sun broke through the clouds. Or maybe not, BJ thought: maybe it was always sunny at Keith Masterly's house. Out his window a vast rose garden appeared, the roses, still blooming away even though it was now September, in every imaginable color, from the palest yellow to a purple so deep it was almost black. There wasn't a droopy or withering petal to be seen—thanks, no doubt, to the army of gardeners moving like guerrilla soldiers among the plants. Out Boris's window a sloping lawn, greener than a golf course, undulated down to the glimmering lake.

The driveway was longer than BJ's street, but the taxi finally stopped, and a man in the same dark-red uniform as the ski-boat driver opened the door on Boris's side. Even after BJ settled the fare, Boris didn't budge. For once in his life Boris was looking a little unnerved.

"Move it," BJ said, giving him a shove.

Grabbing the backpack, he followed Boris out of the cab into the bright sunshine and blinked at a surprisingly unimpressive house: a stucco structure, only one story high, not much bigger than his own house. Nothing like the spectacular showplace they'd seen from the lake.

"Mr. Masterly is on the tennis court," the uniformed man said, opening the dark-red front door.

The two boys stepped inside—and found themselves at the top of a wide redwood staircase. It curved down four or five stories through a vast atrium to a reception room bigger than all of Garfield Middle School, with gigantic plate-glass windows looking out across a terrace and a lawn to the lake and the Seattle skyline. The little stucco house was just a pimple on the real house, a tiny penthouse to gain access to the floors below. On the way down Boris gawked, openmouthed, at the galleries to the left and right, while BJ wondered if this could be the stairway to Sirius he'd heard about for so long.

He also wondered whether "Mr. Masterly" meant Keith Jr. or Keith Sr. The idea of meeting Keith Masterly Sr. filled him with excited dread. But when at last they reached the foot of the stairs, another uniformed man appeared and led them out to a wide terrace overlooking a grass tennis court, where Keith Jr. was about to serve to a beautiful golden-haired woman whom BJ recognized from photos as Keith Sr.'s second wife.

Keith Jr. stopped in mid serve and came rushing off the court and up the terrace steps. "So it is you!" he said, shaking both their hands. "This is so great!"

"We were in the neighborhood and thought we'd stop by to make sure you're okay," BJ said.

"I'm fine, thanks to you guys. Can you stay for lunch?"

"I could eat a horse," Boris murmured.

"Fantastic. I think we're having Dungeness crab."

"Is your father here?" BJ asked.

"This time of day? Never. He's a total workaholic." Keith Jr. turned and squinted at the helipad beyond the tennis court. "The chopper's here, so he's probably at MasterTech. I think he said something about the cinema division. Listen, just let me and Angie finish up. I'm letting her beat me. If you want to cool off in the pool, there's extra bathing suits in the cabana."

"Thanks," BJ said. "But you know what I'd really go for?"

"What?"

"To sit in that." He pointed at the sleek helicopter. "Just for a minute. I've never been in one."

"Knock yourself out," Keith Jr. said.

33

"**F**or heaven's sake, Darryl, it's lunchtime! Are you sick?"

Darryl sat up groggily in his bed and blinked at Ruthie Katz. Between his work on G-17 and his late-night chimney-climbing sessions with Nina, he'd worn himself to a frazzle, and since Mr. Masterly wasn't around, he'd let himself doze back off after this morning's pep talk.

"I guess I slept in," he said sheepishly.

"Well, shake a leg. I need your help."

Darryl dragged himself up and joined the team in the dining hall for lentil soup and turkey sandwiches. After lunch, down on L, Ruthie pulled rank, pressing him into service on an experiment she'd set up in Chem. Her bright idea was to heat up a solution containing her personal favorite element—ruthenium, number forty-four on the periodic table—and shoot it down a tube at high speed into a solution of G-17 in hopes of stabilizing it. But Darryl couldn't seem to wake up completely, and after watching the complicated process fail twice, he rested his head on the counter and dozed off.

"Aren't you getting enough sleep, Darryl?"

It was Mr. Masterly's voice. "I didn't know you were at the lab, sir," he said, conquering an impulse to squirm away as Mr. Masterly laid his hands on his shoulders.

"Just got back. Do you doze off like this often?"

"No, sir."

"Are you eating well, taking your vitamins?"

"Yes, sir."

"You sit up late watching movies?"

"Well, sometimes."

"Hmm. I considered shutting down the audio and video systems at eleven, but there's been so little abuse, I didn't bother."

"But, Mr. Masterly, it's just . . ." Darryl could hear Ruthie out in the octagon, giving Snoodles orders. "I guess the experiment bored me a little."

"Let's see," Mr. Masterly said, picking up a brown jar. "Ruthenium, eh. You don't think it'll work?"

"Not really."

"Have you had any new ideas of your own?"

"Actually, yeah."

"What's that?"

"I was thinking how G-$9\frac{1}{2}$ might be the problem. So I broke it down into two parts. Three in all."

"Did you make some compound?"

"Uh-huh. Yesterday I injected one of the rats."

"And?"

"Um, I forgot to check," Darryl said, not wanting to admit he'd slept the whole morning away.

He got off his stool and led the way to Bio, passing Paul, who was on his way out with a jar of fruit flies. Darryl walked up to the cage containing the crusty old rat he'd injected. The rat had fleecy fur. His eyes were no longer pearly. Instead of a scrofulous gray, his tail was a healthy pink.

Darryl let out a low whistle as Mr. Masterly joined him by the cage.

"Where's the compound?" Mr. Masterly said, his voice hushed.

Darryl pointed at the jar of murky turquoise liquid Snoodles had helped him mix up.

"What dosage?"

"I gave him three cc's. Diluted, of course. One part compound per ten parts saline solution."

Mr. Masterly diluted the compound with saline solution and sucked three cc's into a hypodermic. Then he opened the door to another cage and injected the rat there. He and Darryl stood side by side, their eyes glued to rat number two as Snoodles shuffled in and started sponging off counters.

Long after Snoodles had finished cleaning up and left, Darryl and Mr. Masterly were still staring at the second rat. It must have been half an hour after the injection when Mr. Masterly nudged Darryl with his elbow. "Is it me, or is he getting a little friskier?"

The rheumy old rat had climbed onto his wheel and started to jog. After a minute he stopped, as if to catch his breath. His eyes were clearer; his fur wasn't so wiry and mangy; his feet and tail weren't so discolored. Off he went again, this time at a run. The next time he stopped to rest, he looked as young and vibrant as the rat in cage number one.

Mr. Masterly turned from the transformed rat to Darryl and again laid his hands on his shoulders. In spite of what Nina had said about it being impossible to hypnotize an unwilling subject, Darryl felt himself falling under the spell of the dark, gleaming eyes. Suddenly Mr. Masterly broke into a huge grin. It brought out crow's feet and lines around his mouth, but made his face more appealing than Darryl had ever seen it.

"You're brilliant," Mr. Masterly said, and then he hugged him harder than his father ever had. "Absolutely brilliant." He released him and shouted: "Everyone, in here!"

In a trice the whole team, Snoodles included, was crowding into Bio, Billy carrying a test tube of mercury.

"Look!" Mr. Masterly cried, pointing at the denizens of cages one and two. "These bright-eyed young fellows

were just like those"—he pointed at the decrepit old rats in the other cages—"till they were injected with a new isomer of G-17. And who do you suppose we have to thank for this breakthrough? This ingenious young man right here."

As everyone clapped, Darryl swelled with pride, no longer wanting to squirm out of Mr. Masterly's grasp.

"We're going to have to add a wing to the trophy case just for Darryl," Mr. Masterly said when the ovation ended. "But you've all been working hard. You all deserve a great deal of credit. Take the rest of the day off, everybody."

"Really, sir?" said Ruthie. "What are we supposed to do?"

"It so happens I brought a new movie, straight from MasterTech's cinema division. Get a little exercise and have some dinner, and I'll pop it in for you."

## 34

After a leisurely lunch on the Masterlys' terrace, BJ and Boris got to ride back across the lake in a limousine. The passenger section was like a living room, with plush facing sofas and a TV and a CD player and a phone and a bar stocked with liquor and soft drinks. But what caught Boris's attention was a big jar of macadamia nuts.

"I wouldn't eat that Dungeon crab if I really was stuck in a dungeon," he declared, gobbling nuts. "You'd think with all that dough they'd get something decent like burgers."

"Well, we did what we came to do," said BJ, who'd actually liked the crab.

"That was pretty slick, I gotta admit."

While checking out the helicopter before lunch, BJ had managed to slip the GPS under the pilot's seat. He flicked on the personal tracker now, and a map of the east side of Lake Washington appeared on the screen, a pulsing dot marking the Masterly estate on Hunt's Point.

Halfway across the floating bridge, the limousine stopped, and the driver lowered a tinted dividing window to inform them there was a jackknifed tractor trailer up ahead. BJ flicked off the tracker and flicked on the TV. Boris immediately grabbed the remote, and they spent the next forty-five minutes haggling over which show to watch.

When they got home, at around four, Boris raided the fridge while BJ cleaned out the litter box and fed the cats. BJ then flopped down on the living-room sofa for a snooze, but Boris came in and blasted a cop show on the TV. Rolling over to give him a piece of his mind, BJ felt the personal tracker in his pocket.

He pulled it out and turned it on. The map that appeared wasn't of the east side of the lake, it was of the whole western part of Washington State.

"Check this out."

"Jeez," Boris said, scooting over beside him. "It's way up in the freakin' mountains." The pulsing dot had migrated all the way from Hunt's Point into the northern reaches of the Cascade Mountains. "Think it's that lab place?"

"Maybe. Or maybe he's just on a business trip."

"What kind of business they got up there? It's just rocks and trees and them iceberg things, right?"

"You mean glaciers?"

The front door opened.

"For goodness' sake," Mrs. Walker said, closing the

door behind her. "What are you boys trying to do, wake the dead?"

"Hi, Ma," BJ said, pocketing the tracker and muting the TV.

"Hey, Mrs. Walker," said Boris.

"For the long weekend," she said, depositing some videos on the table behind the sofa. "Gosh, these shoes are killing me."

As soon as she went into her room to change into slippers, BJ dashed out to the Nova and fished a road map of Washington State out of the glove compartment. Down in the basement he and Boris compared the map with the much smaller one on the personal tracker.

"There?" BJ said, approximating the position of the pulsing dot on the larger map.

"Higher," said Boris.

After considerable arguing they managed to agree on where to put an X on the map.

"What now?" Boris said.

"We see where he goes next. Then we mark another X. Then another and another. If he goes back to the same place a lot, it's probably the lab."

"Hey. It's dead."

The screen on the personal tracker had gone dark. BJ picked it up and pressed the On button. Nothing happened.

"Crud. Grimface must have called the cops. They'd call the dealership, and the dealership would call the satellite company."

"You mean after all that work all we get's one lousy X?"

"I guess." After staring at the map for a considerable time, BJ added, "Too bad you left the toolbox at the shelter."

"How come?"

"Might have been useful."

"What for?"

"Breaking into the Kirbys' house on Alder Street."

Boris snorted. "I don't need no toolbox to break into a house."

"You don't?"

"Cripes, no."

## 35

When Darryl steered his movie pod off to the right, the entire Milky Way came into focus, stretching out before him like an endless white-pebble driveway. Down and to the right, he discovered a spiral galaxy in the process of forming. Soon a couple of other pods crowded in beside him—Paul and Ruthie—so he moved off on his own and stumbled on a red giant in the final stages of collapse.

The new movie, *Mastering the Universe*, was a feast. After witnessing the dramatic explosion of a supernova, Darryl entered a solar system with twin suns. He hardly knew where to turn. And fresh wonders kept replacing the old ones. When he guided the pod back through the flickering waters to reinvestigate the Milky Way, he found himself in one of the gaseous tides around a Cepheid. And the spiral galaxy had become the moons of Jupiter, all laid out for him to explore. And the collapsed red giant had become a black hole.

But breathtaking as the spectacles were, Darryl's mind began to wander. This might have been explicable if he'd been worrying about the planned escape on

Monday night. He and Nina had only that night and two more left for training, and neither one of them had yet made it even halfway up the shaft. But he wasn't thinking about the escape. He was reliving his triumph. He could feel Mr. Masterly's fatherly hands on his shoulders, hear the applause. When he submarined through the blue pinwheel in the Triangulum constellation, the stars around him actually seemed to arrange themselves into the atoms of the G-17 molecule.

*Mastering the Universe* was a hit with the rest of the kids. Once Abs let them out of their pods, they all stood around on the pod platform comparing notes, complaining about all the things they'd missed, wishing the movie would run again right then and there. It was well after eleven before they trooped off to their rooms. So Darryl and Nina couldn't meet to train till after midnight, by which time even Hedderly had called it a night and gone to bed. They were so tired, they didn't even attempt going beyond the second seam.

Back in Nina's room afterward they collapsed in her velvet chairs.

"Do you think we'll make it, Darryl?"

"I don't know."

"You still want to escape, don't you?"

He wasn't altogether sure that he did, but he said, "Of course."

"I wish we didn't have to train so late at night."

"Yeah, I know," he said, yawning.

The next day her wish came true. In the middle of breakfast Mr. Masterly's voice came over the PA system, announcing that everyone had the weekend off.

"You've earned it. It's Labor Day weekend, and you've all labored brilliantly. So enjoy yourselves. The new movie will be running continuously."

An enthusiastic cheer greeted this last piece of news, and everyone scurried off to AquaFilm—everyone except Billy and Suki, who went to play tennis, and Nina and Darryl, who headed for the pantry. By lunchtime Nina had reached the fourth seam—her personal best. After lunch Darryl made it to the third, and if it hadn't been for the swarm of butterflies in his gut, he, too, might have made the fourth.

On his way to dinner he was a little disappointed to see no Darryl trophy in the trophy case yet, but a few minutes later a different kind of honor was bestowed on him. Hedderly was just carrying the first platter into the dining room when Mr. Masterly's voice came over the PA again.

"Darryl, I was hoping for the pleasure of your company at dinner. If you'd care to join me, go to the elevator."

Like the time he'd been called down to L, the others

looked gratifyingly jealous—except Nina, who looked distinctly troubled.

"Guess I better go," he murmured, setting his napkin on the table.

As soon as he stepped into the elevator, the door closed, and up it went, swooshing right past E. The door opened on a rosily lit room not unlike his bedroom except that it was over twice as big, with higher ceilings and a spiral staircase in one corner.

"Welcome to my humble home away from home," Mr. Masterly said, stepping in through an archway to a farther chamber. "I rarely have visitors. In fact, I never have visitors. But this is an occasion."

As he approached his host, Darryl's apprehensive excitement turned to stupefaction. Mr. Masterly smiled.

"How old would you guess I am?"

"You barely look twenty-five!"

"A good age, I think. Not too young, not too old."

It was incredible. He'd shed twenty years since yesterday. The bags under his eyes were gone; his complexion had a youthful glow, his dark hair a shiny luster.

"Have a seat, Darryl."

As in the rooms on S, there were two red velvet chairs pulled up to a low table. Mr. Masterly moved a battered briefcase off his chair before sitting down.

"How much did you take?" Darryl asked, eyeing a

vial of turquoise solution on the table.

"Six cc's, diluted ten to one, after breakfast. It took longer to work on me than the rats—a couple of hours. I had another dose after lunch. I'm hoping three a day will keep Father Time at bay."

Mr. Masterly picked up his remote and pressed a button. As music filled the room, he leaned back with a contented smile on his youthful face.

"Do you know *The Well-Tempered Clavier*, Darryl? Johann Sebastian Bach. Now *there* was a man with a deep understanding of time."

"What's a clavier, sir?"

"Good for you to ask. There's no more valuable trait than curiosity. Combine it with a will to conquer and nothing can stop you."

"Then why do they say curiosity killed the cat?"

"Well, I guess it's because everything of true value entails risk. But non-risk-takers are of no interest to people like us, are they?"

Darryl shook his head, wondering what Mr. Masterly would say if he knew the risk he and Nina were going to take on Monday night.

"A clavier," Mr. Masterly said, "is a an old keyboard instrument—an early form of piano. Do you like fish brains?"

"For what?"

"Dinner. Fish have rather small brains, so you need quite a few for a meal, but it's the most refined source of protein there is, and what little fat they contain keeps your skin elastic. I've trained Hedderly to make quite a good fish-brain mousse." Mr. Masterly pressed a button on his wrist gizmo. "Send up two fish-brain dinners, will you, please, Hedderly? And two carrot juices, and a diced spinach salad with tofu."

He spoke far more politely to Hedderly than Ruthie ever did, and before long an amber light on the wall started blinking. Mr. Masterly stepped over and pressed it. Darryl heard a swishing sound, then a panel slid back, revealing a food cart.

"Is that a dumbwaiter, sir?"

"The one exception to my rule of keeping dumb things at a distance," Mr. Masterly said, setting out their dinners. "Eat up."

The fish-brain mousse, which wasn't even warm, tasted like slime, but out of politeness Darryl ate about half of it, washing down each bite with a swig of carrot juice.

"Maybe it's an acquired taste," Mr. Masterly said after cleaning his plate. He took an eyedropper out of the vial and squirted about six cc's onto his tongue. "I did a little homework on you, young man."

"You did?"

"Your first name's not Darryl."

"No, that's really my middle name."

"Your first name's Martin."

"Yeah, after my dad. They named my older brother after my mom's father, so I got named after Dad. Everybody always called me by my middle name to avoid confusion."

"So your initials are MDK."

"Uh-huh."

"My middle name is David."

"So you're KDM."

"Exactly. The reverse of yours. Interesting, no? And you were born almost thirteen years ago. It was almost thirteen years ago that I started planning all this."

A phone rang in the farther room, and Mr. Masterly excused himself to go answer it, giving Darryl the opportunity to squirrel away the rest of his fish brains in his napkin. While waiting for Mr. Masterly's return, his eyes fell on the battered briefcase. It seemed out of place. Everything else in the room was so new and state-of-the-art.

*There's no more valuable trait than curiosity.*

After checking to make sure Mr. Masterly was still off in the far room, Darryl opened the briefcase and pulled out a worn spiral notebook. Scrawled on the cover in faded red ink was the word "MasterPlan."

Underneath this was the month and year of Darryl's birth. He opened to the first page—and for a second thought he was looking at a sketch for the needlepoint family tree that used to hang over the mantelpiece in his grandparents' house. But the branches and leaves of this tree didn't hold the names of his or anyone else's ancestors. Carved into the trunk, like a girlfriend's initials, were the letters CT. Higher up, the trunk divided into three main limbs, each with a word carved into it: Capital, Workforce, Brainpower. Higher up the Capital limb was the word Profits, and above that it branched out into limbs etched with the names of familiar MasterTech games like CastleMaster and CyberJinx. Higher up the Workforce limb was the word Expendable, and above that it branched out into limbs with unfamiliar initials carved into them: WWSMF, CWSMF, etc. Higher up the Brainpower limb was the word Shelters, and the branches above that also bore mysterious initials.

"Sorry about that," Mr. Masterly said, striding back into the room. "Business."

With no time to stick the notebook back into the briefcase Darryl slipped it under his rump and sat on it.

"Seems I'm going to have to make a few calls," Mr. Masterly said. "If you like, you can go down to E and catch the end of the movie."

"Okay, sir."

As Mr. Masterly bussed their dinner dishes onto the cart in the dumbwaiter, Darryl coiled the notebook and slid it up his sleeve, like a sheath around his arm.

"Thanks for dinner, sir."

"I hope it's the first of many," Mr. Masterly said, turning to give Darryl's mop of hair a fond tousling.

**36**

Nina was sitting in room eight listening to her favorite song when Darryl walked in. "Dinner must have been good," she said, narrowing her eyes at him.

"It was yucky," he said, closing the door. "Fish brains."

"Then why do you look so happy?"

He came over and sat in the other chair. "It's my formula, Nina. Mr. Masterly could be his own son!"

"You mean he took it?"

"And it worked!"

"So you'll be world famous," she said, without much enthusiasm. "What's it like up there?"

"Like this, but even fancier."

"Can you get out?"

"I didn't have a chance to explore."

"Want to go train?"

"Um . . . okay. But first I've got to get some food in my stomach. What'd you guys have?"

"Pork chops."

"Maybe Hedderly has some leftovers." He changed into his cross-training shoes and, pulling something from his sleeve, tossed it on his bed. "Meet you in the pantry."

She had to change her shoes, too, but as she got up to follow him out the door, the spiral notebook caught her eye. She picked it up and started leafing through it.

She was still standing there rooted to the spot when Darryl came back half an hour later.

"I've been waiting for you," he said.

She just stared at him.

"What's wrong? You look like a ghost."

"You didn't read this thing?"

"I just sort of glanced at it."

She held it out. He took it and sat down. As he read, the color gradually drained out of his face, so that when he lifted his eyes from the final page, he looked as ghostlike as she did.

"We're done for," he whispered. "And it's all my fault."

"You couldn't know that."

"That DeathMaster game. I should have put two and two together. It was his face getting younger." He tossed the notebook on the table and jumped up. "Come on, we've got to get out of here!"

"How?"

"The vent. It's our only chance."

"But what about the others?"

He considered this.

"It would be like murder," she said.

"Yeah, you're right. But they haven't been training. How could they get up that thing when we can't?"

"I guess we have only one choice."

"What?"

"To take his advice."

"What do you mean?"

"We have fertile young minds. We have to open them up to all the possibilities. Make the new connections."

"New connections," Darryl repeated.

"This is a think tank, right? We've got to think."

## 37

Awakened by a strange noise, Nina groped for her glasses and was astonished to see that it was five P.M. She'd slept the whole day away—all of Sunday!

Then she remembered: she and Darryl hadn't dragged themselves into their beds till almost seven that morning. Mr. Masterly, having given them the weekend off, must have turned off his wake-up recording.

She dressed quickly and peeked out into the corridor. The sound that had woken her was Suki sobbing in the doorway to room five. Nina took her by the arm and led her back into her room and sat her in one of the chairs.

"What's the matter?" she asked, pushing the beautiful hair off Suki's tear-stained face.

"It's so horrible!" Suki said with a gasp.

"What is?"

"Okāsan and Otōsan—Mama and Papa. I never think of them at all!"

"What happened to them?" Nina asked soothingly.

"They were flying to Japan for my grandmother's funeral and the plane crashed." Suki covered her face.

"It's so horrible! And I never give them a thought!"

"It's not your fault, Suki, believe me. It's the vitamins."

Suki dabbed at her eyes with the back of her hand. "The vitamins?"

"They dull your emotions. So you won't think about the past and stuff."

"But . . . but I took mine this morning."

"That was just an aspirin with a little blue dye. I made them up in Chem last night and replaced the real ones before breakfast."

"You did?" Suki sniffled. "Why?"

Nina handed her the MasterPlan, then went out into the corridor and knocked on the door to room six. No one answered, but she opened the door anyway. Greg Birtwissel was sitting in one of his chairs staring at the movie screen. Frozen on the screen was an image of an avalanche.

"Greg?" she said, shaking his shoulder.

He didn't shift his eyes from the screen, didn't even acknowledge her presence. It took her a good ten minutes to coax out of him that his mother and sister had been killed in a rock slide near White Pass. He felt so wretched at having forgotten them that not even hearing about the vitamins brought him around. When she insisted she had something for him to look at, he just sat there, so she had to tug him to his feet and drag him back to her room. They found Suki sitting there holding the MasterPlan in trembling hands, her pretty, almond eyes glazed with horror.

"I know," said Nina, taking the notebook and passing it on to Greg.

"What should we do?" Suki said in a hollow voice.

"We better round everyone up. I'll check the rooms if you'll check E and L."

Half an hour later the whole team, except for Darryl, was gathered in room seven. They were a pretty cheerless group, and nobody's spirits were lifted by reading the MasterPlan. Ruthie could barely decipher it because her eyes kept tearing up at the thought of her parents, both of whom had died cruel deaths from cancer.

"What's this?" she sniffled, pointing at the CT on the trunk of the tree.

"You ought to know," Nina said. "You say it every morning."

"Conquering Time?" Ruthie wiped her eyes with her sleeve and pointed to the initials in the high branches of the Workforce limb. "What are these?"

"The asylums where he got the people to build this place. CWSMF. That's Central Washington State Mental Facility."

"What happened to them?"

"The workforce? They were expendable."

"Expendable?" Greg squeaked.

"Except for Abs and Hedderly and Snoodles. He kept them on as staff."

"You mean he killed the rest?" Ruthie said.

"It doesn't say. Maybe he lobotomized them and sent them back to the loony bins."

"And what are these?" Ruthie was pointing to the higher branches of the Brainpower limb.

"The shelters. It's pretty ingenious, really. He picks orphans, with no family to care about them."

"You mean we're expendable, too?" Ruthie said.

"Once we serve his purpose."

"But whoever discovers the way to stabilize G-17 will be more famous than Albert Einstein and Isaac Newton and Christopher Columbus rolled into one."

"I wouldn't count on it," Nina said.

"You mean . . . ?"

"Read the last page."

Ruthie gave her eyes a good mopping and read the last page. When she finished, she looked as ghostly as the rest of them.

"We'll be blown to smithereens," she whispered. "But . . . but it won't happen till . . . How long have you been off the vitamins, Nina?"

"Quite a while."

"And what have you been doing?"

"Lately we've been training—Darryl and I. Climbing a vent in the pantry. We just wanted to escape. We had no idea what was in there."

"Well, we're okay as long as Mr. Masterly doesn't have what he wants. We can plot our escape. Or plan a rebellion. I just hope Darryl's formula doesn't work on people as well as it does on rats."

Nina lowered her eyes. "That's the trouble. It does."

"You mean it worked on Mr. Masterly?" Suki gasped.

"I'm afraid so."

"What!" cried Ruthie.

"Where is Darryl anyway?" said Billy.

"Yeah," said Mario. "Where's the traitor hiding out?"

"You mean executioner," Ruthie said grimly.

"He's got us killed!" Greg shrieked.

"He didn't know," Nina said.

"Where is he?" Mario demanded.

"Sleeping," said Nina, who'd poked her head into room eight a few minutes ago. "He and I were up all last night planning our escape."

This news seemed to lower the anti-Darryl voltage in the room.

"What's the plan?" Ruthie said.

"Wait here. I'll get him."

Just as Nina shut the door to her room behind her, the panel lit up at the end of the corridor. She barely managed to shrink behind the trophy case before the elevator door opened.

Firm steps sounded in the corridor. An amazingly youthful version of Mr. Masterly passed by her and gave the door to room eight a firm rap.

"Darryl?" The familiar voice chilled her. Mr. Masterly opened the door. "Napping, eh? I guess you need to catch up, after all your brilliant work. Listen, why don't you come up and have a bite of dinner with me? Get dressed, I'll wait."

Pressed back between the wall and the case, Nina trembled so violently she was afraid the trophies would start to rattle. Had Mr. Masterly missed the MasterPlan? Was he inviting Darryl upstairs to poison him?

## 38

**D**arryl wondered exactly the same thing as an oyster slithered down his throat.

Once again he was sitting across from Mr. Masterly up in the private penthouse, and once again dinner—raw Hood Canal oysters—was about as slimy as could be. But the texture of the food was the least of his concerns. It was taking all his concentration just to hide his nervousness and keep his eyes off the battered briefcase by Mr. Masterly's chair and the vial of turquoise liquid on the table.

"Do you remember the day we met?" Mr. Masterly said after swallowing his half-dozenth oyster.

"It's a little hazy," Darryl lied. "At that shelter place?"

"Mmm. I mentioned adopting you as my son. I've been thinking. I'd really like to."

Despite everything, Darryl felt a spark of gratification. But then he remembered: *expendable . . . self-destruct mechanism . . .*

"How would you feel about me as a father?"

"It would be . . . an honor."

"Excellent. Shall we go?"

"Go? Where?"

"Home."

"To Hunt's Point? Is it close enough to walk?"

"I'm afraid we'll have to fly."

"How?"

Mr. Masterly pointed at the spiral staircase. "That takes us to my helicopter."

"You mean right now?"

Mr. Masterly wiped his mouth and tossed his napkin down by his plate. "No time like the present."

"But I'd have to pack."

"You won't need PL clothes anymore."

"But what about . . . my notes. I'd need to collect my notes."

"What notes?"

"On G-17. And some other things I've been fooling around with in my spare time."

"Really?" Mr. Masterly took a thoughtful sip of mineral water. "You know, maybe morning would make more sense. I want to collect a few things myself—and to be honest, I prefer flying in daylight. Tell you what. I'll wake you at dawn. But one thing. If you happen to run into any of the others, don't mention you're leaving. It's our little secret."

Darryl nodded.

"Now don't stay up late watching movies in bed, okay?"

"Okay. Mr. Masterly?"

"Yes?"

"Could I have an apple to take with me?"

"Of course."

There was a bowl of fruit on a shelf in the dumb-waiter. As Mr. Masterly reached in for an apple, Darryl snatched the vial off the table and replaced it with an identical one from his jumpsuit pocket.

"Fresh from Yakima," Mr. Masterly said, handing the apple over. "First of the season."

## 39

**W**hen he got back down to S, Darryl went straight to Nina's room and found the whole team there.

"Are you okay?" Nina asked anxiously.

"I'm not sure," Darryl said. "I had to eat three oysters."

"Ick," said Greg, making a face.

"Did he notice it was missing?" Nina asked.

"I don't think so."

"What did he want?"

"To adopt me."

"Adopt you!" Ruthie cried.

"Adopt you?" Nina said.

"He's going to wake me up early to leave," Darryl said.

"You're going with him?" said Suki.

Darryl took a bite of his apple. It was tart and crisp and got rid of the lingering fishy taste in his mouth. He ate the whole thing, then dropped the core onto the floor and said: "Let's get out of this dump."

Without another word he headed for the door. Nina was right behind him, and the others fell over themselves following.

"Where are we going?" Ruthie cried as they headed down the corridor.

Darryl led the procession into the kitchen, where Hedderly was sitting on a stool, peeling carrots.

"Come with us, Hedderly," Nina said.

Grinning, Hedderly wiped his hands on his apron and followed them out to the emergency stairs. Up on E, Abs was cleaning the pool with a long-handled skimmer.

"Abs, could you please give us a hand?" Darryl said.

Nodding enthusiastically, Abs dropped the skimmer and followed the parade under the AquaFilm archway. Nina and Darryl stepped onto the escalator and motioned for the others to follow.

"You want to go to the movies when we're about to be blown to bits?" Billy asked, getting on behind them.

"Nope," Nina said. "We want the pods."

"What for?"

"You'll see."

Thanks to the air tanks, which served as ballast in the water, the pods were very heavy. Abs was able to heft one up in his arms, but Hedderly needed help from Mario, and it took all the rest of them combined to lift a third. It required four trips to get all dozen pods down the escalator and through the gym and down the elevator to the octagon in L.

When they came gasping out of the elevator with

the last three, a sleepy-looking Snoodles shuffled out of his room in slippers and a nightshirt and a striped nightcap.

"Better change, Snoodles," Darryl advised. "It might be a chilly night."

"Y-yes, y-young sir," Snoodles said, shuffling obediently back into his room.

"Hedderly, could you go back up to S and get us some provisions?" Nina said. "Water and fruit and nuts and stuff?"

"Provisions for what?" Ruthie asked as Hedderly trooped off.

"For if we get out of this place," Darryl said, opening the door to Chem. "Abs, could you bring one of the pods in here?"

Abs hefted a pod and followed Darryl to the rear of Chem.

"In there," Darryl said, pointing at the mixing tank.

Abs set the pod in the tank. Soon Hedderly returned with a bulging sack of provisions, which Darryl had Abs cram into the pod.

"Snoodles?" Darryl called out.

The whole team had crowded anxiously into Chem to watch, but they made an aisle so that Snoodles, now in his regular lab coat and pants, could shuffle up to the tank.

"Water, please," Darryl said.

Snoodles attached a hose to the nozzle of a gray tank marked "$H_2O$" and started filling the mixing vat. When the tank was half full, Darryl gave a signal and Snoodles switched off the valve. Darryl sealed the pod, which was floating like an egg-shaped canoe in a cistern, and hit the button on the tank's outer wall. As when Snoodles mixed up G-17, the vat's bottom dropped out. The pod vanished.

"Ew!" cried Greg, as eye-stinging disinfectant swirled around the tub.

"Where did it go?" cried Ruthie, as the bottom of the tank flipped back into place.

"Who knows?" Darryl said. "But it's bound to come out somewhere. We figured the water would make the trip smoother. Abs, could you please bring in another one?"

Abs lugged in a second pod and set it in the tank.

"All set, Nina?" Darryl said.

They'd decided last night that she should be first to go—the human guinea pig. She climbed onto the edge of the tank, and as Snoodles filled it up, Darryl helped her into the pod. After fastening her seat belt, she looked up at him, her innocent blue eyes big behind the lenses of her glasses, and his throat suddenly constricted, so that his "Good luck" came out as barely a whisper.

"You, too," she whispered back.

He took a deep breath, sealed the lid, and flipped the flush switch. *Whoosh!* Just like that, Nina was gone. Though it felt as if she'd taken half his insides with her, he cleared his throat and said:

"Ready, Ruthie?"

"No way!"

"You want to stick around here and die?"

By the time Abs set another pod into the tank, Ruthie was ready to climb in. Again Snoodles filled the tank halfway. Darryl sealed the pod and hit the flush switch.

One after the other he flushed them down the tank: Paul, Billy, Mario. After Suki he had to rinse his eyes, they smarted so much from the disinfectant fumes.

"Ready, Greg?"

Greg cowered back into the shadows.

"Then you're next, Snoodles."

As Abs picked up the elderly man and slipped him into the waiting pod, Darryl assumed the filling duties. After Snoodles came Hedderly, who took up even more of the pod than Paul had, though he didn't seem to mind the cramped space a bit. The last thing Darryl saw of him was a huge grin, as if he was going on one of the rides in the Seattle Center.

"It's now or never," Darryl said, turning to Greg.

"Abs has to go second to last, and I have to go last."

"Why do you get to go last?" Greg whined.

"There'll be nobody to seal the last person in. So I'm going to try to hold the lid closed with my hand. Unless you want to do that."

Greg stepped up shakily and climbed into the third-to-last pod as Darryl started refilling the tank. When Darryl secured the lid, Greg started pounding the hard plastic, his eyes nearly popping out of his head in panic. Darryl knew all too well how that felt, but it didn't keep him from flipping the flush switch.

"Bring both the last two, will you, Abs?"

Abs lugged in a pod and placed it in the vat. When he fetched the last one, Darryl had him set it upside down on the tank's edge.

"We couldn't have done it without you," Darryl said, shaking one of Abs's powerful hands.

Abs could barely squeeze himself into the pod in the vat, but once in, he sat docilely scrunched up, watching like a faithful dog as Darryl filled the tank. Darryl sealed the lid and hit the flush button.

For the last hour Darryl had been forcing himself to act bravely and decisively to inspire the others with confidence. But the instant Abs vanished, the instant there was no one left to put on an act for, he started trembling like the night he'd climbed into the tree hut.

The truth was, the prospect of falling into a mysterious pipe in a transparent pod terrified him.

Still, he didn't have much choice. He put his trembling hands onto the last pod and pushed. It tumbled into the vat, landing right side up. He half filled the tank, turned off the water valve, and climbed into the wobbly canoe. His arm wasn't quite long enough to reach the flush button on the outside of the tank.

"Here, let me. After all, I owe you a double debt now."

Out of the shadows stepped the new, younger Mr. Masterly. With one hand he hit the flush switch; with the other he grabbed Darryl by the scruff of the neck. The pod was sucked down—but not Darryl. For a moment he simply dangled over the abyss, his eyes stinging painfully. Then Mr. Masterly yanked him over the edge of the tank and set him on his feet beside him.

"Interesting. I feel as strong as when I was twenty-five. The middle-aged me might have dropped you—and then where would we be?"

Darryl couldn't speak. He could barely breathe.

"I don't know how I'll ever repay you," Mr. Masterly said, patting him on the shoulder. "First you come up with the formula. And now you spare me all this trouble. Not to mention the guilt."

Darryl could only blink in bewilderment.

"What do I mean? Simply that you did the disposal job for me."

"You mean . . ." Darryl swallowed hard. "You mean the pods won't come out somewhere?"

"They'll come out all right. But the lab's deep in the wilderness. The pods are unbreakable and airtight and can't be opened from inside. When their oxygen runs out, they'll all suffocate." He smiled ruefully. "I'd gotten attached to you all, so I really wasn't sure I'd be able to go through with it. Now I won't have to."

## 40

**W**hat with the free ride home from Hunt's Point in the limo, Friday's expenses hadn't been nearly as steep as BJ had feared, so that night he splurged and took his mother to dinner at her favorite Italian restaurant, Basta Pasta, up in Montlake. At his insistence the waiter brought her a glass of Chianti with her spaghetti, and Mrs. Walker, who rarely drank, got a little giddy. She hooted when BJ sprang his idea on her.

"Hiking! What in the Sam Hill put that idea in your head, sugar pie?"

"School starts next week, Ma. I haven't been anywhere all summer. Hiking's cheap. Boris wants to try it, too."

"Don't you need equipment? Tents and such?"

"That's the best part. Dare's folks had all that stuff. He wouldn't mind me borrowing it."

"You mean going over to their house? I'm sure it's all locked up. I imagine the bank will be auctioning off the contents and putting the house on the market."

"That's the thing, Ma. I was walking by there the other day and these people were clearing out the garage, and I said how I was Dare's friend and they let me take some of the hiking gear."

"You're not serious."

In fact, he was stretching the truth considerably, but he nodded and said, "It's all down in the basement."

"Good heavens. Where would you want to hike? Discovery Park?"

"Not in the city! We want to go to the mountains."

"But how would you get there?"

"Don't you get it? We want you to come, too. You'd drive us."

She hooted again. "Me! Hiking?"

"Think how great it would be. We could drive up to a nice campsite tomorrow and set up a tent—like a home base. We could cook out, and you could bring some books and stuff. Then maybe Boris and I could hike up a trail and spend a night on our own, just so we could get a taste of the wilderness."

"By yourselves?"

"You could come, too, if you want. That'd be great. I just wasn't sure you'd be into hiking ten or fifteen miles uphill."

"You're talking about this weekend?"

"Sure. The weather's supposed to be great—and

Monday's a holiday. And like I said, next week school starts."

"High time," she murmured.

"Don't you think it would be cool, sleeping in a tent?"

"Why people want to sleep on the ground when they have perfectly comfortable beds at home is beyond me."

"Aw, come on, you've got to open your mind to new things. Knowledge is the ship to the Hesperides, right? There's other kinds of knowledge than what you get out of books."

"I don't think I need to sleep on the ground to know I wouldn't like it."

"Well, maybe we could borrow the Bottses' RV. Then you could sleep in a bed."

"But why on earth do you want to go way up in the mountains, sugar pie?"

"Think of the Sunday book. Those Greek gods lived up on a mountain. And Moses went up a mountain to get those commandments. And the Dalai Lama lived way up in the mountains. And Noah's ark landed on a mountain. And the Japanese worshiped Mount Fuji. And the Incas had their holy city way up in—"

"Okay, okay. I suppose I haven't given you a vacation this summer. I suppose Clara would come over and feed the babies."

When they got home, the "babies" were all

crouched around the perimeter of the kitchen, eyes fixed coldly on Boris, who was sitting at the table gnawing the last of a leftover leg of lamb off the bone. Boris set it down and wiped the back of his hand across his mouth.

"Beege said I could have it."

"That's fine," Mrs. Walker said. "But I thought you were going back to the shelter."

Such was the story BJ had come up with.

"They're full up," Boris said. "So I came back here. Hope it's okay."

"It's perfect," BJ said. "That way we can get an early start in the morning."

"But I thought we locked up the house before we left," Mrs. Walker said.

Boris looked to BJ, who put on a sheepish face and said:

"I might have left the back door unlocked. Sorry, Ma."

Mrs. Walker went into the hallway and opened the door to the basement.

"Lands," she said. "You *did* get a mess of hiking gear."

BJ slipped Boris a low five.

"Piece of cake," Boris said under his breath.

Later on, when the boys were alone in the basement,

BJ found out that amassing the heap of knapsacks and coiled ropes and furled tents and rolled-up sleeping bags had required two trips to First Hill.

"But it was no sweat," Boris said. "A baby could've broken into that place. Ever seen that REI store by the freeway?"

"Sure," said BJ, whose winter boots were from Recreational Equipment Inc.

"Their basement looked like that."

"What are these for?" BJ asked, picking up a bundle of aluminum stakes wrapped in twine.

"You got me."

"Ever put up a tent?"

"You kidding?"

"Me neither." From under a canteen BJ pulled a bunch of geological survey maps and a book: *The Joys of Mountaineering*. "Smart you grabbed this."

"Yeah, well, you're the big reader."

And indeed long after Boris was snoring away in the bottom bunk, BJ was still reading about rappelling and belaying and top roping.

## 41

"**I**'m wiped," Boris declared, dumping his backpack on the ground.

He sat down on it and lit up. But even though they'd been hiking the whole day with thirty pounds on their backs, and even though the last couple of miles, up a winding, wooded notch, had been the steepest part of all, BJ remained on his feet, staring out across the clearing before them. It was stippled with reds and yellows and blues: wildflowers that seemed to be lit from within, thanks to the slanting, late-afternoon sunlight. But it wasn't the candlelike flowers that grabbed his attention, it was the rock face rising up beyond them. It went straight up about a hundred feet, sheer as a ten-story building.

"What?" Boris said, blowing dragonlike streams of smoke out his nostrils. "That cliff thing?"

"You think it's a cliff?"

"What else?"

"It's too . . . too square. Like a building."

"But it's all rocky."

BJ dumped his pack and tromped through the

wildflowers. Except for its squareness, the rock face fit in well enough with the sort of wilderness they'd been slogging through all day. There was a cave a little way up the cliff with water trickling out into a little stream, which he was able to jump across easily enough. Higher up the face were a couple of rocky ledges with twisted pines growing out of them. Still, there was something eerily unnatural about the thing as a whole.

As he started to reconnoiter around the base, Boris fell in at his side.

"Think it might be the lab place?"

"I don't know."

When they got halfway around the buildinglike mountain, Boris called out: "Neen?"

The only reply was a faint echo off the rock.

"Darryl!" BJ cried.

They called the names over and over but got only echoes in response.

"I don't see no doors or windows," Boris said. "Or any of those heliport things."

"Maybe he lands on top," BJ said.

By the time they'd circled the monolith, the sunlight had deserted the clearing, dulling the wildflowers. The two boys refilled their canteens in the little stream and, weary to the bone, plunked down on the ground by their packs.

"What do you think?" BJ said.

"You're the big thinker," Boris replied, hugging himself.

"You cold?"

"Uh-uh. It's just freakin' creepy up here."

"It's beautiful."

"It's just a bunch of rocks and trees."

"You like Skid Row better?"

"At least there's people there. There's nobody here but us."

"Not if that lab thing's in there."

Boris lit up another cigarette. "You want to know what I think?" he said, blowing smoke in BJ's face.

"What?"

"Masterly was probably flying to Spokane or something and found that GPS thing under the seat and tossed it."

"I don't know," BJ said, watching the last sunlight desert the pinnacle. "I think we should climb it."

"In the friggin' dark?"

"In the morning."

"You'll never get your fat butt up there."

"We'll have to stick in pro and secure ropes."

"What?"

"Stuff from in here," BJ said, pulling *The Joys of Mountaineering* out of his pack.

Boris reached into his own pack and pulled out a package of hot dogs.

"We got to pitch the tent before we eat," BJ said.

"No way."

"You need light for pitching a tent. At least if you've never done it before."

Last night they'd slept in beds in the Bottses' RV. They'd borrowed it yesterday morning, picked up supplies at the QFC, and headed east across the floating bridge. Mrs. Walker had assumed they wanted to go somewhere like Mount Rainier National Park, but BJ had insisted on *real* wilderness, and they'd ended up at an obscure campsite off Route 20 in the Northern Cascades Wilderness Area—about ten or twelve miles south of the X on his map. This morning Mrs. Walker had changed her mind about letting the boys go off for a night on their own, but BJ had begged so pitifully and relentlessly, crossing his heart that they'd be back by two sharp the next day, that he'd finally worn her down. In spite of perfect weather the wilderness experience hadn't lived up to his expectations. Not only were their packs heavy, they'd had to stop over and over to compare the readings on the Kirbys' electronic compass with the geological survey map onto which he'd transferred the X from the road map. Every time he decided they should go right, Boris wanted to go left—except when they'd finally crossed a meadow and found the notch that had led them up here. This had been posted with "Keep Out!" and "No Trespassing!" and "Private Property" signs, and for Boris the idea of going where you weren't supposed to had been irresistible.

*The Joys of Mountaineering* advised digging a moat around your tent in case of rain, but it took them the rest of the daylight just to set the thing up, and since the sky was clear, they skipped the moat in favor of building a fire and roasting hot dogs. After taking a swig from his canteen, Boris spat the water on the ground.

"I knew those beer commercials were full of it," he said. "Always saying how these mountain streams are so friggin' fresh."

BJ sampled the water and spat it out, too. It had a chemical taste.

"See?" Boris said. "And no mustard. I can't believe you forgot the mustard."

"I was trying to cut out as much weight as possible."

"Hot dogs with no mustard. It's like them low-tar cigarettes."

After dinner they put the fire out, and while Boris smoked, BJ brushed his teeth by the funny-tasting stream. He'd originally cut out the weight of his tooth-brush and toothpaste, too, but his mother had shoved

them into one of his pack's side pouches and made him promise to use them.

The tent barely had room for their packs and their two sleeping bags. They unrolled the bags so that the head of one was at the foot of the other. The temperature had dropped quite a bit since sunset, so they wormed into their bags with their clothes on.

"When was the last time you took a bath?" BJ asked.

"I don't take baths. But look who's talking about smelling."

They each had a flashlight, and while Boris read the steamy paperback he'd stolen from Ms. Grimsley's handbag, BJ pored over *The Joys of Mountaineering*.

"I think we can do it," he declared after a while.

"Do what?"

"Climb that cliff. It doesn't really matter if it's ten feet or a hundred feet. It's the same idea. What you do is you stick these whatjamajiggies in the cracks and—"

At a splashing sound from the nearby stream BJ instantly flicked off his flashlight.

"What the . . . ?" Boris said as BJ flicked his off, too.

"Shh. Might be a bear."

There was a series of splashes.

"Do bears go around in herds?" Boris whispered.

"They're good at sniffing out food, that much I know. Did you wrap up the extra hot dogs?"

Boris dug in his pack. "Yeah, they're wrapped up," he whispered. "Can they smell *us?*"

How could they not, BJ thought. He heard a click, horribly close. "What was that?" he whispered.

"I ain't going to be dinner for no bears."

The flap let a paper-thin shaft of moonlight into the tent, enough for BJ to make out the glint of a blade. "You went in my drawer?" he hissed, recognizing the switchblade.

"Your drawer, my knife."

"Sneak. I ought to—"

"You ought to be glad I brought it."

"A lot of good it's going to do against a bunch of bears."

But the splashes had subsided, and after about half an hour their fatigue conquered their fear and they fell fast asleep.

## 42

"**Y**ou really should thank me, Darryl."

Mr. Masterly was leaning on the computer console in the octagon, but Darryl, though only a few feet away, barely heard him. His ears were still ringing with echoes of what Mr. Masterly had said in Chem: *The pods are unbreakable and airtight. . . . When their oxygen runs out, they'll all suffocate.* Thanks to him, Nina and the others would plop out into some no-man's-land and watch each other die.

"How were you planning to close the lid of your pod?"

Darryl just stared dolefully at the white marble floor. First he'd wished his family dead, and they'd died. Now he'd killed off Nina and all his other lab mates.

"If you thought you were going to hold the lid down from the inside, it never would have worked. There's toxic chemicals in the flush, and it would have been a very bumpy ride. You'd have been contaminated. So you see we're indebted to each other."

What he needed, Darryl realized, was Mr. Masterly's special elevator key. With that he might be able to get up to the roof and the helicopter. Maybe he could figure out how to fly it down to the pods before the oxygen supplies ran out.

"Tell me, what did you think of my plan?" Mr. Masterly said.

Darryl stared at the man's pants pocket, wishing he could will the key out of it into his hand.

"I found it missing when I was packing up a few things I didn't want to leave behind. Lucky for you— otherwise I wouldn't have come down till morning. Where is it, by the way? It has sentimental value to me."

When Darryl didn't answer, Mr. Masterly glanced around the gleaming octagon.

"Kind of a shame, isn't it, getting rid of all this? But it wouldn't do to have some granola-eating hiker stumble across it. And I must say it's served its purpose beyond my wildest expectations."

Darryl cowered as the new, younger Mr. Masterly approached him.

"I'm not going to bite you, Darryl. I just want to shake your hand."

Darryl didn't offer his hand, but Mr. Masterly took it anyway, giving it a good squeeze.

"By all rights your name should end up in the history books. *Darryl Kirby: The Boy Who Conquered Time.*" Mr. Masterly sighed. "I doubt it will. Chances are, I'll get the credit. Though you never know. If I decide to keep our little discovery to myself, *nobody* will get the credit. Which would be selfish and selfless at the same time, I suppose. . . . In any event, I want to thank you. And say I'm genuinely sorry you decided against being my son."

It was such a relief when Mr. Masterly finally let go of his hand and went back into Chem that Darryl just stood there taking deep breaths, not even thinking of fleeing. Soon Mr. Masterly came back out with some papers under his arm and a big brown jar in his hand.

"Lifetime supply of the new G-17," he said. "Though perhaps not for my particular lifetime. Lucky I know how to make more."

He walked across the octagon and got into the waiting elevator.

"Good-bye, Darryl," he said.

"But . . ."

"Yes?"

"But what about . . . ?"

"What about you? I really am sorry. But you do have the run of the place."

Run of the place? But how long would it be a place? As the elevator door closed, Darryl's eyes shot to the panel over the door. The elevator stopped at S. Would he be looking to recover his MasterPlan? It was in Nina's room.

Darryl bolted into Chem and grabbed a jar of hydrochloric acid off one of the shelves. As he carried it up the emergency stairs, he unscrewed the lid so he would be ready to throw the contents into Mr. Masterly's eyes. But when he stepped into the corridor on S, the elevator door was once again closing on Mr. Masterly's youthful face.

Up above, the S panel went dark, and the E panel lit up. But only briefly. The elevator proceeded straight to the top floor.

Darryl set the jar of acid down carefully on the floor and hustled to the elevator. Pushing the button did nothing: the elevator remained at the top floor. Darryl dashed into the kitchen and got the big metal spoon Hedderly used for stirring soup and tried to use it as a crowbar. He'd once seen a movie where the hero gets to the top of a building by shinnying up elevator cables. But Paradise Lab was far too solidly constructed. The elevator door wouldn't budge.

Darryl clattered back down to L, darted into the back of Chem, and hit the flush button on the mixing vat. The cleanser shot out the nozzles and swirled around the shiny sides as the bottom flipped open. But he just watched, paralyzed by the knowledge that he would never come out alive. How could a corpse open the pods?

The elevator still wouldn't leave the top floor, so he took the stairs back to S, where he ducked into his room and changed into a black jumpsuit and his cross-training shoes. From there he headed straight for the pantry and climbed into the dumbwaiter. It didn't move. He pressed the button outside the door. Nothing happened. It must have been for bringing the dumbwaiter back down when it was up at Mr. Masterly's private quarters, or else for making the little amber light up there start blinking.

The sight of the vent across the dim pantry made him feel faint, so he went into the kitchen and ate a hunk of leftover meat loaf. Back in the pantry he pulled the vent cover off and squeezed into the shaft on his back. At the end of the long tube there was no moon, no stars, only a circle of charcoal gray that looked about the size of a nickel. He shut his eyes tight, trying to get a grip on his dread—and Nina's face appeared, her eyes big and terrified behind the lenses of her glasses, her lips mouthing the words "Help me!"

Then Nina turned into his brother. "*Why do you have to be such a wuss, Dare?*" Jason said, shaking his head in disgust.

## 43

**B**J had no idea how long he'd been asleep when a new noise woke him. Not a splashing this time but a loud tapping from somewhere very near the tent.

"What the heck is that?"

Boris groaned, rolling over in his bag. More tapping ensued, till there was a whole symphony of it.

"What the freak is it?" Boris said, sitting up.

"Woodpeckers?"

"Bears and woodpeckers hang out together?"

BJ leaned forward and gingerly pulled back the tent flap. Between them and the monolith a trail of what looked like enormous eggs glimmered in the moonlight.

"What the heck?" Boris said.

As they gaped out, one of the eggs started rolling toward them. It came to rest against a rock no more than ten feet from the tent.

"Is that one of them dinosaur eggs?" Boris said.

"Isn't that a kid inside?" BJ said.

"Jeez. Maybe it's one of those MBO things."

"You mean embryo? It's awful big for an embryo."

"Maybe it's from Mars or something. Maybe that

square mountain's a UFO."

As the tapping started up again, BJ grabbed a flash-light and shone the beam on the nearby egg.

"I don't think embryos have shoes," BJ said. That's what the boy in the egg was using to tap with.

"How do you know what they got on Mars?"

"He looks like a regular kid. Maybe he's one of those bubble boys who's allergic to everything."

"Looks more like blubber boy to me."

The boy in the egg *was* pudgy.

"Looks like he's trying to get out," BJ said. "Maybe we should—"

"No way! That's how it always starts. You let one out, then they take over the whole friggin' world."

But the bubble boy looked so unthreatening—kind of pathetic, really, shoehorned into the egg, gasping for breath—that BJ squirmed out of his sleeping bag and crawled out of the tent with his boots and flashlight. At the sight of him the bubble boy gestured violently toward the top of his egg. There was a lever on the outside.

BJ pulled on his boots and walked hesitantly toward the other eggs. They were beached in the shallow stream. One was empty, the lid open, but the others were all closed. One contained a big sack; the others, people: three grown-up men, three girls, and three boys. The girls and boys were all gasping and gesturing desperately to be freed. The adults were gaping out, dazed.

Darryl turned his flashlight back on the fat boy in the egg nearer the tent. His face was turning greenish. It really looked as if he was suffocating. But as BJ walked back that way, Boris popped out of the tent, switchblade in hand.

"No way, José."

BJ sighed. "We've been through this before, Boris."

"Yeah, but I ain't fallin' for no stupid tricks this time."

"Fine. Kill 'em if you want."

"Huh?"

"Look at him. He's suffocating in there. They are, too." BJ turned and swept his flashlight across the other eggs. He settled on one. "You know, she looks kind of like you. Just a lot prettier."

"You think I'm falling for that?" Boris said contemptuously.

BJ shrugged but kept the beam of his flashlight on the girl, who was knocking on the inside of her egg with her shoe. "Maybe it's *not* your sister. In that picture you showed us, she didn't wear glasses."

At this Boris turned and looked along the beam of BJ's flashlight.

"Neen!" he screamed.

He dropped the knife, sprinted to the egg, and wrenched open the lid. The girl popped up, gasping.

"Neen!" he cried, hugging her.

She just gasped, her chin resting on his shoulder.

"Neen! I found you!"

He yanked her out of the egg and set her on her feet. But instead of resting in his arms, she pushed him away and ran jerkily, one shoe off, one shoe on, right toward BJ. Did she want to hug him, too? Or maybe smack him?

She passed right by him as if she didn't even see his dark face in the moonlight. She virtually threw herself on the bubble boy's egg, using her shoulder to push the lever. The lid opened, and out popped a plump, greenish face.

"Thanks," the fat boy sputtered.

But she was already gone, racing toward the other eggs.

"Help!" she cried. "They're almost out of air!"

BJ and Boris joined in, releasing lid after lid. They shied away from ones containing grownups, a couple of whom were awfully big, nearly filling their eggs. But Nina didn't hesitate to set the adults free.

"Is everyone okay?" she cried when all the eggs were hatched.

"This guy's out cold," BJ said of a skinny boy he'd pulled out of one egg. "Did you guys come out of that cave up there?"

"I guess," said Nina, glancing at the rock face.

"Then you fell ten or twelve feet. Lucky more of you weren't knocked out."

The others were rasping for air, collapsed on the fronts of their eggs. A tall girl soon stood up. "I can't believe we made it!" she cried.

"But where are we?" a Hispanic-looking boy bawled.

A man who could have been the strong man in a circus stood nodding his head, grinning. Another man, kind of a hulk, said, "Thanks, kiddo," while the other man, who was old and stooped, said, "Whew, that was really s-s-something!"

"Was all of you in that lab place?" Boris asked, returning to Nina's side.

"We sure were," said the tall girl.

"What a ride!" gasped an Asian girl with long, glossy-black hair. "It was like the water slide at the Puyallup Fair."

"I chipped a tooth," said the Hispanic boy.

"Ten more seconds and I'd've been a goner," said the fat boy.

"Me, too," said a pimply-faced boy.

"How was you thinking you was getting out of those eggs, Neen?" Boris asked.

Nina looked at the last egg, the one that hadn't been occupied. "Darryl was just going to hold his closed. Then he was going to let the rest of us out."

"Where is Dare?" asked BJ, who'd been shining his flashlight from face to face.

No one answered. Slowly, they all turned and stared up at the gloomily looming rock face—all except for Boris, who stood grinning at Nina. He gave her a conspiratorial nudge as he rolled up his sleeve.

"Together again," he whispered, tapping his NABATW tattoo. *"Nina and Boris against the world."*

## 44

Nina felt as if her heart was being torn in two. After all these months she was finally reunited with her brother. Yet at the same time the boy who'd become a second brother to her was suddenly missing.

As she stared up at the cave in the rock face, the broad-shouldered black boy came up to shake hands.

"I'm BJ. A friend of Darryl's."

"He talked about you," she said. "You and your mother."

"Do you think he fell out of his egg or something?"

"Could be," Ruthie said, joining them. "It was a pretty rough ride."

"I'll go check," Nina said. "Boris and I can—Boris!"

Boris had lit up a cigarette.

"I don't believe you!" Nina cried. "Mom dies of emphysema, and here you are, at it again!"

Boris dropped the cigarette, shamefaced, and ground it under his shoe. Nina stooped down, pulled his pack out of his sock, crumpled it up, and shoved it in her pocket. "Come on," she said.

At the rock face Boris let her climb onto his shoulders. But even then she couldn't reach the cave, and the surface of the rock below the opening was slick and slimy from the trickle of flushed chemicals.

"Abs!" she cried.

Dim though he might be, Abs didn't need to be told what to do. Squatting down, he turned himself into a human stepladder. Boris, with Nina on his shoulders, climbed onto Abs's thighs. Abs then grabbed Boris's ankles, one by one, and placed his feet on his shoulders. Slowly, carefully, Abs raised himself out of his squat.

"Good going!" BJ said as Nina pulled herself into the cave.

"What'd you expect?" Boris said. "We're the Flying Rizniaks."

"Could I borrow that, please, BJ?" Nina called down.

BJ handed his flashlight to Abs, who handed it up to Boris, who tossed it up to Nina. Shining it into the cave, she saw that it was really a twisty drainage pipe. As she hiked up it, using a sort of side-to-side duck walk, the odor from the trickle of liquid between her feet grew more and more intense till it stung her nostrils like ammonia. When her hands started to sting, too, she wiped the slime off on the legs of her jumpsuit.

At the end of the conduit a drop of liquid tapped

her on the top of her head. She peered up forlornly at the bottom of the dripping mixing vat, shut tight as a drum.

By the time she got back to the mouth of the cave, she was desperate for fresh air. Boris was still waiting on Abs's shoulders, and she climbed down lickety-split.

"No sign of him?" BJ said.

She shook her head ominously as she handed back his flashlight. "He must be stuck in there with Mr. Masterly."

"Keith Masterly's in there?"

"Uh-huh. And now that he's got what he wanted, he'll take off and blow the whole place to kingdom come."

"What's he got?" BJ asked as Greg Birtwissel, who'd regained consciousness while Nina was in the cave, started backing away from the cliff.

"That's a long story," Nina said. "But take my word for it, we have to get Darryl out of there."

"How?"

"I wish I knew."

"Maybe brainiac'll think of something himself," said Boris. "Where's Masterly's chopper?"

"On the roof, Darryl told me," said Nina.

BJ swept the beam of light up the forbidding rock face.

"Gosh, that's a long way up," Suki said.

"What'll happen if we're standing down here when it blows?" Billy wondered aloud.

They all exchanged anxious glances—except for Greg, who by then had backed halfway to the woods.

## 45

In his sixties Darryl's grandfather had suffered from a condition that made him shake, especially his hands, but Darryl was shaking far worse than his grandfather ever had. He was at the fifth seam in the vent, and every muscle in his body was on fire, screaming: "Give up!" But even louder was the voice of his conscience yelling, "They'll all suffocate!"

Somewhere around the seventh seam his brain simply shut down, leaving only panting, aching, shaking, and clawing. His knees felt as if they'd been flayed, his wrists and ankles felt as if they'd been smashed with a sledgehammer. His throat was as dry as sand. But his instincts kept him from looking down, and a strength he never would have dreamed he possessed—perhaps he didn't, perhaps it was somehow sent from his dead parents—kept him from letting go.

Then everything went black.

When he came to, his torso was collapsed on something flat and his legs were still dangling down the vent. He was gasping like a fish on a dock. Merely opening his eyes took a monumental effort. When he managed to, he saw a spider, a glistening black one, crouched in the middle of a web. The spider was six inches away and appeared poised to jump in his face, but Darryl didn't have the energy to do anything about it. The web, glazed with moonlight, was stretched between the high side of a metal cone and the lab's sandpapery roof. The cone seemed to have been meant to cover the vent like a hat, but it must have been blown or knocked off quite a while ago, for the web was as intricate as a MondoGameMaster maze.

The spider evidently decided against jumping in his face, and after a couple of minutes Darryl mustered the strength to lift his head high enough to look over the cone. Parked about thirty yards away, half hidden under a camouflaged tarpaulin, was a helicopter as sleek and glistening-black as the spider. Next to it was what looked like a parking meter—though it was awfully hard to imagine anyone giving out tickets here.

Managing to turn his head the other way, Darryl saw a legion of mountain peaks silhouetted against a subaqueous sunset. Poised above the watery western horizon was a waferlike moon that made him think of Nina. The last thing he felt like doing was moving, and the last place he wanted to go was the edge of the roof, but he had to find out if she and the others had made it out of the lab. He wormed forward till his legs were out of the vent. Once his feet were up on the roof, worming was a little easier.

When his head poked out over the edge of the roof, his heartbeat doubled. But dizzying as the sheer, hundred-foot drop was, there was a fantastic payoff at the bottom. Not only had the pods gotten out of the lab, his friends had somehow gotten out of the pods! There they were, scurrying around down below in the moonlight.

"Hello!" he yelled.

Or at least tried to yell. His throat was too dry to produce more than a whisper. He swallowed a couple of times and managed to do better.

A beam of light swept up the rock face and hit him full in the face, blinding him. An echoey chorus of familiar voices washed over him.

"Darryl!"

"Hey, kiddo!"

"Dare, is that you?"

The last voice electrified him.

"BJ?" he cried.

The light left his face. He blinked. Down below the person holding the flashlight turned it on his own face.

"BJ!" Darryl cried, recognizing his friend instantly.

"Hey, Dare!"

"But . . . but what are you doing here?"

"We came to find you! Me and Boris!"

"Hey, brainboy!"

Darryl was stupefied. By some miracle BJ and Boris had found the lab and been there to open the pods! He could see the glimmering pods strewn around a little stream. Farther on, he made out an orange tent remarkably like his parents'.

"You climbed the vent?" Nina called up.

"Yeah!"

"Is there a chopper up there?" Boris yelled.

Before he could answer, a vibration ran through the roof, reminding him that there was still someone else in the lab.

"Turn off the flashlight!" he yelled down. "Ditch the tent! Get in your pods!"

They appeared to obey him. BJ and Boris quickly dragged the tent and their hiking gear into the woods while the others jumped into their movie pods. Squirming back from the edge, Darryl saw a razor-thin sliver of light slant up into the sky about halfway between him and the helicopter. The sliver turned into a beam, and a chilling apparition appeared in it: Mr. Masterly's head. The upper body soon followed, then the complete, youthful man stepped up onto the roof, a suitcase in one hand, his battered briefcase in the other.

Darryl wouldn't have been surprised if Mr. Masterly had walked over and booted him over the edge, but as the shaft of light from below shrank and disappeared, Mr. Masterly turned the other way, toward the helicopter. He yanked off the tarp and tossed his bags into the cockpit. Before climbing in himself, he walked over to the parking meter in the eerie moonlight and seemed to feed it a coin.

Still overheated from climbing the vent, Darryl actually appreciated the rush of cool air when the rotors started up. The spider didn't: he curled into a tight ball in the center of his billowing web. On liftoff everything went black. The tarp, which Mr. Masterly hadn't bothered to tie down, had blown over them.

By the time Darryl writhed out from under it, the helicopter was hovering beyond the edge of the roof, a searchlight aimed straight down. Once Mr. Masterly had assured himself that the escapees were stuck in their pods, the helicopter zoomed off toward the dying light in the west.

Darryl got up and limped, ankles throbbing, over to where the shaft of light had appeared. He had no more luck prying open the sliding roof panel over Mr. Masterly's spiral staircase than he'd had with the elevator door.

He started back toward the edge, then did an about-face and limped over to the parking meter. It wasn't a parking meter. Instead of a slot for coins there was a keyhole, just like in the top elevator button. Above it was a digital readout—dark red numbers glowing like embers: 9:14, 9:13, 9:12.

Darryl wasted only three seconds getting back to the edge. His lab mates were all climbing out of their pods, and BJ and Boris had emerged from the woods.

"Get out of here!" Darryl screamed. "The whole place is going to blow in less than ten minutes!"

A skinny figure already halfway to the woods quickly disappeared into them. But to Darryl's horror the rest of them stayed put.

"Get going!"

At this BJ and Boris took off into the woods as well. But BJ soon returned, lugging a big coil of rope. Surely they weren't going to try to scale the cliff! Not even Darryl's parents could have climbed a rock face as steep as this one.

"Don't!"

But it was a pathetic attempt at a yell.

Boris soon came back out of the woods, too. He was carrying a branch, which he took a knife to, shaving off the bark. He quickly whittled it into a spear and gouged a hole in the thicker end like the eye of a needle. BJ stuck one end of the rope through the hole and tied it off and handed the spear to Abs. Abs backed up about ten yards and heaved the spear into the air.

Strong as he was, the spear didn't get halfway to Darryl before the weight of the uncoiling rope pulled it back down to earth.

"Get out of here!"

But now Darryl could barely even hear himself. Whether it was the strain of the chimney climb, or his vertigo, or the prospect of being blown up—his voice was gone.

Boris went back into the woods and returned dragging the tent. While he gashed it, Nina untied the rope from the spear, then Boris tied something else to the spear while BJ tied something to the rope. Nina handed the spear to Abs, who backed up a few yards again and threw the spear straight up into the air.

This time, to Darryl's astonishment, it came right for him. In fact, he had to pull his head back to keep from being skewered. The spear reached its apex about twenty feet over his head, then clattered down onto the roof. It lay there for a moment, then rolled off the edge. Darryl poked his head back out in time to see it shatter against a rock down below.

"You've got to grab it, Dare!" BJ cried.

They ran to find a new branch and whittle another spear for Abs to throw. Again he managed to heave it onto the roof of the lab on his first try, and this time Darryl pounced on it. Tied through the hole was a piece of nylon thread: unraveled tent.

"Pull it up!" BJ cried.

Darryl pulled on the thread. It grew heavier and heavier, and eventually, instead of thread, he had rope.

With the helicopter gone, the only place to secure the rope was the "parking meter." He dashed over to it and knotted the end around it as the readout wound down: 4:33, 4:32, 4:31 . . .

When he poked his head back out over the ledge, everyone down below started waving and hollering.

"Come on, Dare!" cried BJ.

"Hurry up, Darryl!" cried Nina.

But as he peered down the length of rope, slithering like a hundred-foot python in the breeze, he knew it was useless. It was too far, and he'd used up all his strength on the chimney climb.

"Get out of here! There's only four minutes!"

But his words came out as feeble croaks.

He wormed back away from the edge and struggled to his feet. With his back to the precipice, he took the rope in his sweaty palms, his heart feeling like a bird about to burst out of its cage. He closed his eyes—and saw Nina, who would be buried in the rubble when the lab blew.

Then Nina's face became his father's.

"Come on, Dare," he whispered. "You're the only Kirby left."

Opening his eyes a slit, Darryl started backing toward the edge, feeding the rope out through his oily hands.

## 46

**B**J's hands were sweaty, too, as he steadied the end of the rope, as *The Joys of Mountaineering* instructed. Feeling the rope jerk, he looked up and saw a small, moonlit figure starting down the ten-story cliff.

"He don't look so hot," Boris said.

"How could he after that chimney climb?" said Nina.

"After what?" Boris said.

"What if the whole place blows?" said the Hispanic-looking boy.

"Guess you better make a run for it, Mario," Nina said.

Mario looked over his shoulder, then back up at Darryl. He stayed put.

Except for the one kid who'd already skedaddled, they all stayed put: three adults with scars on their foreheads and eight kids standing there with their necks craned. They all gasped when Darryl lost his grip on the rope. But after a short fall he caught on the branch of a twisted pine growing out of the side of the cliff.

"Careful!" Nina screamed.

"You can do it!" BJ yelled, wishing he could take Darryl's place up there.

"Just don't look down!" Nina advised.

As Darryl continued his jerky descent, the rope slipped in his hands again. This time his foot caught on a little ledge.

"Jeez," Boris said. "He's not going to make it."

"Come on," BJ said, handing the rope off to Nina.

To get a hundred feet of nylon thread they'd had to unravel only a small part of the tent. BJ told everyone to grab hold of the rest of it.

"You know, like when somebody's jumping off a building in a cartoon."

The group formed a circle with the tent stretched out in the middle like a trampoline. The skinny boy who'd taken off shouldered in beside BJ to take his place holding the net.

"Greg!" Nina said. "You came back."

"Well, he got us out," Greg said in a quavery voice.

Darryl must not have taken Nina's advice about not looking down. He must have seen what they were up to, for as soon as the net was tight as a drum, he pushed off the cliff and released the rope. Greg's squeal was still echoing in the night air when Darryl landed on his back—"Oooomph!"—in the middle of the tent.

He looked dazed, but as they lowered him to the

ground, his eyes were open.

"Are you okay, Dare?" BJ cried, kneeling beside him.

Darryl blinked and said something, but too faintly to hear. BJ put his ear up to Darryl's mouth. As soon as he made out the croaked message, he passed it on:

"We've got to get out of here!"

"Come on, everybody, let's go!" Nina cried. "Abs, grab Darryl!"

Abs tossed Darryl over his shoulder like a gunny-sack, and off they all went, abandoning the tent, rope, sack of provisions, knapsacks, and plastic eggs. Fortunately, BJ didn't leave his flashlight. The notch bristled with fir trees that totally blocked out the moon-light. As they were clambering down the twisty trail, someone screeched, and BJ turned and shone his light on the Asian girl, who'd tripped on a root and was hold-ing her ankle. The big man in kitchen whites picked her up and carried her over *his* shoulder, chortling as her long hair tickled his face.

BJ had led them only a couple of hundred yards down the trail when someone kicked him in the small of his back with a heavy boot. At least that was how it felt as he dropped to his knees. A split second after the concussion came a deafening explosion, and the flash-light flew out of his hand. The sudden darkness rang with the splintering *thunks*. Groping, he located the flashlight under a fern and shone it around frantically. The first thing he stopped on was a grinning Abs, standing upright behind him on the trail, Darryl still over his shoulder. Behind him, the tall girl was sprawled on the ground, spluttering as she spat dirt off her lips.

"Is anyone hurt?" came Nina's voice from farther back.

"My shoulder!" whined one boy.

"My knee!" whined another.

"My elbow!"

It turned out that almost everyone had a bruise or a bump or an abrasion, but the soldierly firs had shielded them from the debris of the explosion. Not one of them was seriously injured. Still, they were all too shaken and weary to go much farther in the dark, so BJ and Boris led the way down to the meadow they'd passed on the hike up. It was a brisk night, but dry, and they all curled up together like a litter of puppies under the starry sky.

## 47

"It's an important experiment, Darryl," said Mr. Masterly, standing beside him in Chem. "It may hurt a little, but afterward you can take some G-17, and your skin will be young again. Go ahead, try it."

As Darryl stuck his right hand over the flame of the Bunsen burner, he yelped—and his eyes popped open. He wasn't in Chem at all. He was lying in tall grass under a dove-gray sky. The none-too-soft pillow under his head was one of Abs's calves. Nina was curled up in a ball beside him, her glasses lying in the grass, one of the lenses broken.

Darryl sat up without waking either her or Abs. The meadow glistened in the soft dawn light—or at least the dew in the tall grass glistened. It was pretty chilly, but his right hand felt scalding hot. That's what had awakened him. His palm was bright red. Rope burn.

His ankles were still sore from the chimney climb, but he got to his feet and hobbled around the circle of sleepers, taking a head count. Everyone present and accounted for—except Mr. Masterly, who'd flown away in the helicopter.

"Hey, everybody, wake up!"

A dozen heads lifted from the ground. He'd gotten his voice back.

"He might fly back to make sure we're dead."

"Huh?" said Boris, rubbing his eyes. "Who?"

"You could be right," said Ruthie, who didn't need to be told who "he" was. "We shouldn't be out in the open like this."

"He must have heard the explosion from the helicopter," said Billy.

"Yeah, but he's a careful man," said Nina, putting on her half-broken glasses. "Let's get out of here."

"Anybody have anything to eat?" Boris asked.

"Yeah, I'm starved," said Paul.

Hedderly pulled something out of a pocket: a packet of yeast for bread making.

"I got hot dogs in my pack," Boris said. "I'm going back."

"Are you nuts?" BJ said. "It'll be buried under a ton of rocks. Let's go. Ma's waiting at base camp."

"You go ahead," Boris said stubbornly. "I'll catch up."

Nina tried to talk him out of it, but it was no use, so she went back up the trail with him while the rest of them headed down. Thanks to Darryl's ankles and Paul's knee and Snoodles's age, the larger party didn't move very quickly, and after about four miles Nina and Boris rejoined them in a clearing by a river.

"I hate to admit it, Beege," Boris said, "but you were right."

"It's just a big pile of rubble," said Nina. "Paradise Lab's Paradise Lost."

"Good riddance," said Suki.

"G-g-good riddance," echoed Snoodles.

As if to underscore this sentiment, the morning sun peeked out over the shoulder of a peak off to their left.

Thanks to their early start it was still morning when they reached the campsite. As BJ led them toward the parking lot, where two campers and a big beige-and-green RV were parked, Darryl stared at a young couple frying eggs outside a tent. They reminded him so much of a photo of his parents on their honeymoon hike that he had to fight an urge to cry. The young couple stared right back—for Darryl and the rest of them made a pretty odd procession. Except for BJ and Boris, all the kids were in space-age jumpsuits, while the three adults had crescent-shaped scars on their foreheads.

When they reached the RV, BJ went in alone. Darryl heard Mrs. Walker's "Sugar pie!" through the screen door. In a minute BJ hopped back out. His mother followed but stopped in the doorway.

"What in the name of Pete?" she said, agog.

"Hey, Mrs. Walker," Boris said, sniffing the air. "Is that bacon? I could eat a friggin' horse."

Mrs. Walker stood there in her purple UW sweat suit, blinking in the sunlight. "Who in the world are . . . honey child!"

"Hi, Mrs. Walker," Darryl said, stepping out of the crowd.

She came down the two steps and folded him in her arms. "Is it really you?"

"It's me," he said.

She smelled wonderful—coffee and bacon—and suddenly he couldn't hold his tears back. But she held him long enough that he managed to wipe them away on her sweatshirt. Then she took him by the shoulders and peered into his face.

"Where in Sam Hill did you come from, child?"

"Up there," he said, cocking his head to the north. "We all came from the lab."

"The lab? What lab?"

"We're starved, Ma," BJ said. "How about we drive down to that pancake house we passed? We'll explain everything."

"Yeah!" Boris cried.

"But who are all these people?" Mrs. Walker said.

"This here's my sister, Nina," Boris said, pulling Nina forward.

"You broke your glasses, sweetie," Mrs. Walker said.

"It's okay," Nina said. "Nice to meet you."

"Where'd you get the RV?" Darryl asked.

"It's the Bottses'," Mrs. Walker said.

"If you don't mind," said Darryl, "could we all get in? We don't want to be seen."

"What in the world are you talking about?"

"Pile in!" BJ said. "Ma, I'll sit up front and explain."

But the front seat wasn't divided from the rest of the RV, and as Mrs. Walker guided the lumbering vehicle back down windy Route 20, everybody joined in telling her about Paradise Lab and the great escape—everybody except Abs, who sat doing stretching exercises in a corner, and Boris, who raided the little fridge. However, it wasn't easy to convince Mrs. Walker of the existence of a luxurious, multileveled laboratory embedded inside a mountain.

"I'm sorry to doubt you all," she said. "But how on earth could you build something like that way up here in the wilderness?"

"Using people like Abs and Hedderly," Nina said. "A whole construction crew handpicked from the mental institutions Mr. Masterly backs with all his donations. It's all in his MasterPlan. Isn't that right, Hedderly? Didn't you help build the lab?"

"That's right, kiddo," Hedderly said.

"That's r-r-right," said Snoodles. "I just w-w-wish I could r-r-remember it. I'm s-s-so s-s-stupid!"

"No, you're not," said Ruthie.

Mrs. Walker braked, and they fell in behind a slow-moving logging truck. "But what happened to the rest of this construction crew?" she asked.

"I don't like to think about that," Darryl said.

"It must have taken them ten years to build," Ruthie said, "because he started almost thirteen years ago. Mario and I were the first kids there, and I don't think it's been three years."

"And he just blew it all to bits?" said Mrs. Walker.

"It was like an atom bomb!" Greg said.

Boris didn't contribute to the general conversation till he heard that they were passing up the pancake parlor.

"But I was psyched for a plate of those silver dollar guys!" he cried.

"We can't all troop into a public place," Ruthie said. "Mr. Masterly might have spies."

"I want pancakes!"

"Hedderly makes buttermilk pancakes every Thursday morning," Greg pointed out. "Can you make them on a Monday, Hedderly?"

Hedderly nodded, grinning, and Mrs. Walker made a pit stop for the ingredients at a small grocery store in the town of Newhalem. Soon they were back on the road with Hedderly whipping up skillet after skillet of silver-dollar pancakes on the RV's range. Darryl ate seventeen—third most after Boris (nineteen) and Paul (twenty-two)—after which he passed out on the plaid sofa.

"Wake up, Dare. We're home."

Darryl rolled over onto a sore elbow and blinked at BJ. "Home?" he said groggily.

"Come on."

The two of them were the only ones left in the RV. Stumbling after BJ to the doorway, Darryl saw that they were pulled up in front of the familiar little sky-blue house. Here in Seattle it was raining, but instead of going into the house Darryl stood on the sidewalk feeling the drops on his nose and the back of his neck, staring at the pretty little rock garden, the neatly painted shutters, a bicycle left out on the lawn next door. In spite of the rain a robin was hopping around the grass near the bike, listening for worms. Over the rooftops a seagull was wheeling in the woolen sky, dirty-white against gray.

His stupid eyes pooled up again.

"Welcome back, buddy," BJ said, draping an arm over his shoulder.

Darryl wiped a sleeve of his black jumpsuit over his

face. "I want to go see my old house," he said.

"Sure, that's probably a good idea. I'll go with you tomorrow."

"I don't have a key."

"We'll take Boris."

Darryl gave BJ a sidelong look.

"He broke in on Friday," BJ said. "Where do you think we got the ropes and stuff?"

"Huh," Darryl said, opening his hand to let the cool rain hit his raw palm.

"That hurt?"

"Sort of. But in a way it feels good."

"Come on, we're getting soaked."

Darryl let BJ pull him up the path through the rock garden, but he stopped again before they reached the front door.

"What is it, bro?"

"Just . . . how'd you ever find the lab?"

"Later for that. It's a long story."

"Well, however you did it, I've got to thank you."

"You'd have done the same for me. What are best friends for—right?"

Darryl grinned. "Right," he said, holding out his raw hand to shake.

"Later for that, too," BJ said. "Come on."

48

What with a dozen people and a half dozen cats squeezed into the living room, there was barely room for Darryl and BJ.

"Listen up, everybody," said Mrs. Walker. She was standing in front of the TV, facing the rest of them. "From what I've heard, it sounds as if you're all pretty much alone in the world. And after what you've been through, you must be feeling awfully disoriented. I wish to goodness I could take you all in. I really and truly do. But as you can see, it's impossible. So what I'm going to do is call Ms. Grimsley and—"

"Not Grimface!" BJ cried. "No way!"

"She works for Child Protective Services, sugar pie. I'll bet she has enough beds in the shelter to—"

"She works for Masterly, Ma."

"He's right, Mrs. Walker," Darryl piped up. "If he finds out we're alive, we're done for."

"I think you're being a bit melodramatic," Mrs. Walker said. "But if you really feel that way, then I'll have to call the police. Or maybe I should call Henry Botts first. . . ."

"We ought to lie low and find out what's happening with Mr. Masterly," said Nina.

"Couldn't they stay with us for a while at least?" BJ said.

"I could cook," said Hedderly.

"I'm g-g-good at cleaning," said Snoodles. "And Abs could do the y-yard work."

Abs nodded eagerly.

"This kitty's darling," said Suki, who was stroking Galileo. "We had two Siamese at home."

"I think we should all stay together," Greg said, sniffling.

"Yeah," Mario and Billy chimed in.

"We could join a think tank and pay you rent," said Ruthie. "We're all smart."

"You'd all have to sleep standing up, dear," Mrs. Walker said ruefully. "I'm afraid it wouldn't work."

"What if we got a bigger house, Mrs. Walker?" Nina suggested. "One with lots and lots of bedrooms. With a nice view of the water."

Mrs. Walker laughed, her whole body jiggling. "I'm a librarian, sweetheart. Librarians don't make much money."

Nina stepped up to her, reached into a pocket of her jumpsuit, and set something on top of the TV. Peering around Hedderly, Darryl saw that it was a crumpled pack of cigarettes.

"Do you smoke, dear?" Mrs. Walker said.

"Of course not," Nina said, dumping something else on top of the TV.

Hedderly leaned forward, blocking Darryl's view. Mrs. Walker gasped.

"Where'd you get 'em, Neen?" Boris cried, squeezing up to the front.

"From down on L. I grabbed them just before I got in my pod."

"L?"

"You don't mean to say they're genuine?" said Mrs. Walker.

Darryl saw Boris hold up something small and glittery to the light: one of the diamonds Mr. Masterly had brought them to study. "Sure looks real," Boris said.

"They're the best quality money can buy," Nina said. "Put it back, Boris. They're for Mrs. Walker."

Boris, who'd already pocketed the stone, made a face as he put it back. Craning his neck around Hedderly's shoulder, Darryl was delighted to see that there was a whole heap of diamonds.

"You could buy a mansion with those, Ma," BJ said.

"You could buy a friggin' skyscraper," Boris said.

"Way to go, Nina!" Greg cried. "Now we can stay together!"

"W-why didn't I think of it?" Snoodles said, bamming

his skull. "I'm s-s-such a knucklehead."

"I didn't think of it either, Snoodles," Ruthie said, putting an arm around the old man's bony shoulders. "I'm sorry for ordering you around all the time. It was those darn vitamins."

"I'm sorry for always making you get me seconds, Hedderly," said Paul.

"I'm sorry for never getting in touch with you and BJ, Mrs. Walker," Darryl said.

"Jeez," Boris said. "If we're having a sorry-fest, I'm sorry for ripping off your GameMaster."

"What did you do with it?" Darryl asked.

"Sold it."

"Boris!" Nina cried.

"I used the money for bus tickets, for cripe's sake. I was looking for you."

"Really?" Nina said.

"What do you think?" He made another face as Nina put an arm around him, but he didn't squirm away. "I'd never have thought to take a bus up to that lab place, though. Beege came up with the GPS idea. Hey, did I tell you we went to Masterly's house?"

But the name Masterly cast a pall over the room.

"What if he finds out we're alive?" Greg whispered.

"Don't you worry—nobody's going to lay a hand on you," Mrs. Walker said. "This is a free country."

"He's awful rich and powerful, Ma," BJ said.

"If you're all telling me the truth, we can have him arrested," Mrs. Walker declared. "I'll have Henry build a case against him."

"I wish I'd brought his MasterPlan," Darryl muttered. "That would be good evidence."

"Maybe we could find it in the rubble," Nina said.

"Nah, he took it."

"I wonder if the explosion made the news," Ruthie said. "Or was it too far away from everything?"

Mrs. Walker turned on the TV. A man in a chef's hat appeared on the screen, demonstrating a food dicer.

"Will you look at that!" Hedderly said, wide-eyed.

After the commercial the six-o'clock news came on. A woman with stiff-looking blond hair reported that she was filling in for the regular newscaster, who would be back from vacation tomorrow.

"Our top story this Labor Day is the oil spill in Alaska, where teams of conservationists are working round the clock to save as much of the wildlife and waterfowl as possible. But closer to home we have a strange story unfolding—a very strange story. Last night a helicopter crash-landed twenty miles east of Seattle, just north of Lake Sammamish, narrowly missing a roadside tavern called the Stop On Inn. Three patrons and the bartender went out to try and save the pilot.

They had to use a crowbar to jimmy open the door to the half-mangled cockpit—and all they found inside was an infant boy. KING-TV has just gotten an exclusive interview with Chuck Lundquist, one of the men on the scene."

Darryl was smiling to himself as a red-faced man with a gap-toothed grin appeared on the right half of the screen.

"Tell us, Mr. Lundquist, what do you think became of the pilot?"

"Beats the heck out of me," the man said, poking at his ear piece.

"Could the pilot have escaped before you arrived at the scene?"

"Houdini couldn't have got out of that thing."

"What's your theory then?"

"I ain't got no theory. We pries open the door, and there's this little nipper sitting strapped into the pilot's seat."

"What was he wearing?"

"You could barely make him out. He was all swallered up in one of them *Star Trek* outfits, big enough for me. Darnedest thing you ever saw."

"May I ask what you do for a living, Mr. Lundquist?"

"Logger. Laid off, at the moment."

"Were you drinking last night prior to the crash?"

"We'd all had a couple. But nobody'd tied one on or nothing like that."

"Interesting. Thank you for taking the time to speak with us, Mr. Lundquist."

"Any time, lady."

Mr. Lundquist disappeared as the newscaster took over the whole screen again.

"There you have it. And in another bizarre twist, KING News has learned that the helicopter belongs to none other than Keith Masterly, founder and CEO of MasterTech. As yet KING News has been unable to get a comment from Mr. Masterly himself, but a spokesman for the company informs us that the helicopter was probably stolen. As for the infant 'pilot,' he remains in a coma in Sammamish Hospital. The doctors there hold out little hope—though of course even if the infant lives, he won't be able to enlighten us as to the circumstances of his presence in the helicopter. Also found in the cockpit were a briefcase and a suitcase, but the authorities have yet to disclose their contents. KING News will keep you updated on this unlikely story as more details come in. . . ."

The newswoman moved on to the upcoming primaries for Seattle's mayoral election, and Mrs. Walker flicked the TV off. By then no one was watching it anyway. They were all gaping at Darryl.

"Well," Darryl said. "Looks like he took it."

"What did you do?" Nina asked.

"While you were making the fake vitamins, I was mixing up an a new batch of G-17. The first batch was ten parts saline solution to one part compound. This one was full strength. I switched vials when I went up to his room last night. He must have taken his after-dinner dose, and a couple of hours later . . . well, I guess it kicked in."

"What on earth are you talking about, child?" Mrs. Walker said.

"It's kind of complicated," Darryl said.

"You mean that baby was Mr. Masterly?" Greg squeaked.

Darryl nodded.

"You're kidding me," said BJ.

"Nope."

"Way to go!" cried Billy, slapping Darryl on the back.

"Hooray!" Paul and Suki cried in unison.

"Good thinking, Darryl!" said Ruthie.

Mario held up his hand for a high five, but when Darryl showed him his raw palm, Mario contented himself with giving him another smack on the back.

"I wonder if the MasterPlan was in the briefcase," Ruthie said.

"Whether it was or not," said Nina, "I don't think we have to worry about Mr. Masterly anymore."

"I don't understand a single word of this," said Mrs. Walker.

"I don't either," said BJ.

"Me neither," said Boris. "But if Neen's happy, I'm happy."

"Excuse me, Hedderly," Nina said.

Hedderly moved aside so Nina could get to Darryl. As Darryl's eyes flicked back and forth between her good lens and her broken lens, his mind flicked back and forth between now and the night she'd shown him the vent: the night they'd seen the moon.

"Looks like we made it, huh?" he said.

Her face broke into a bright smile, making it quite pretty; then she leaned forward and gave him a kiss, making his face as hot as his rope-burned hand.